Why Must a Black Writer
Write About Sex?

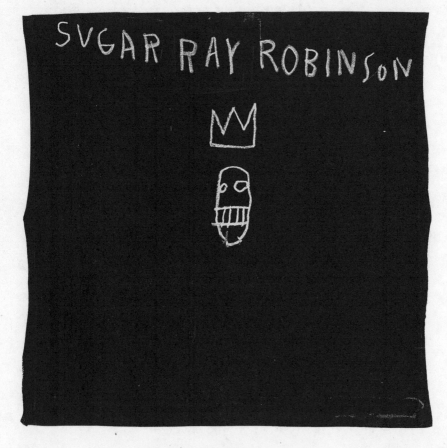

Jean-Michel Basquiat, UNTITLED (SUGAR RAY ROBINSON)
Acrylic & oilstick on canvas, 1982
© *The Estate of Jean-Michel Basquiat*

Why must a
black writEr
writE about
sEx?

Dany LafErriErE

translatEd by David HomEl

COACH HOUSe PReSS

Cover Illustration:
Jean-Michel Basquiat, detail of UNTITLED (SUGAR RAY ROBINSON), 1982.
© The Estate of Jean-Michel Basquiat. All rights reserved.
Courtesy Robert Miller Gallery, New York NY.

This is a work of fiction. All references to real persons, living or dead,
or to characters resembling real persons, and all actions and statements
attributed to such persons, are products of the author's imagination
and have no basis in fact.

Published with the assistance of the Canada Council, the
Department of Canadian Heritage, the Ontario Arts
Council, and the Ontario Publishing Centre.

Coach House Press
50 Prince Arthur Avenue, Suite 107
Toronto, Canada M5R 1B5

FIRST EDITION
2 4 6 8 10 9 7 5 3
Printed in Canada

Canadian Cataloguing in Publication Data
Laferrière, Dany
[*Cette grenade dans la main du jeune Nègre est-elle
une arme ou un fruit?* English]
Why must a black writer write about sex?
Translation of: *Cette grenade dans la main du jeune
Nègre est-elle une arme ou un fruit?*
ISBN 0-88910-482-4

I. Title. II. Title: *Cette grenade dans la main du jeune
Nègre est-elle une arme ou un fruit?* English.

PS8573. A44C413 1994   C843'.54   C94-931746-2
PQ3919.2.L34C413 1994

I'm not denying my origins,
but I just don't get along with other Blacks.
There's more to life than being Black.

—A graffito in the New York subway

To the novelist James Baldwin
The musician Miles Davis
The painter Jean-Michel Basquiat
All three casualties of America
War rages in the New World.

Writing in North America

I

This is not a novel. As I write these words, I think of René Magritte painting a pipe and adding the caption, "This is not a pipe."

This book is composed of field notes I took throughout North America. In a train headed for Vancouver with a fat woman across from me who kept staring in my direction, thinking I was drawing her portrait (she was right). In a Greyhound bus flying south towards Key West, one sunny Friday, with the intense blue ocean on both sides of the bridge. In a vegetarian restaurant in San Francisco where I couldn't eat because of a greasy, microscopic thing stuck to the corner of a tall skinny girl's mouth, a few tables away. In a taxi outside a Manhattan disco at three o'clock in the morning, desperately seeking bagels. In the bathroom at Shades (a Montreal bar patronized by young actresses with metallic breasts who shoot you laser looks), with a girl with green hair bitching because she couldn't find the right vein to pump herself full of poison. In

America, you've got to move. American space is an invitation to speed.

II

An influential East Coast magazine commissioned a long piece from me. They were putting together a special issue on America, or so they said.

"What do I care if America is four or five or six hundred years old? I'm forty and I'm not making a big deal about it."

That's what I told the brother who tracked me down in my Miami hideaway.

"Fuck America, man. The money's green, and there's plenty of it. Take it, because if you don't, somebody else will."

"Why me?"

The usual stupid question people ask.

"I suppose you must be the flavor of the month."

"And?"

"They were looking for you everywhere, and now they've found you."

"What about you?"

A short silence fell.

"Let's just say that I've already been the flavor of the month."

"When was that?"

"Three or four months ago."

"That's all it lasted?"

"Things happen fast here."

"What do they want from me?"

"I'm not too sure. I suppose they want a black who's not from here, but who knows the neighborhood, if you get what I mean."

"Why don't they get a real American black?"

"An African-American, if you please. The name changed again."

"If you have to look to words for your identity ... Anyway, why not one of them?"

"Probably because they don't want the hassle. They don't want some guy who's going to turn everything into a black man–white man kind of thing."

"Forget it, then, because that's the only thing that interests me."

"I know you," he said with a laugh. "You're into the black man–white woman thing."

"That's one way of examining the issue."

"Why not? But this is for the leisure section. And if you don't talk about money, whites don't think it has anything to do with them."

"You mean the rich."

"Cut the Marxist comedy, man. Here, white equals rich."

"I hate commissions."

"Don't worry, do whatever you want ... Remember, you're the flavor of the month. You bum around a little, they pick up the tab, you write down your impressions. Take it from me, man, their checks don't bounce. That's America," he concluded in a peal of bitter laughter.

"They really respect writers that much?"

"Are you bullshitting me?"

"Not at all."

11

"They want to get the issue out. The whole thing's completely underwritten by the Ford Foundation, and the Getty Foundation, and the Mellon and the Morgan and the Rockefeller Foundations. It's just a tax write-off anyway, man, so don't take it too seriously. They want to make a big splash, and they're ready to pay the price."

"What should I do?"

"You call them back and tell them you're in."

"It sounds like a call-girl trick."

"The principle's the same," he told me, then hung up.

III

It's not every day that one black writer turns another black writer onto something good, and by that I mean a project that might bring in a little cash. I called back. They wanted someone they could cut a good deal with. That's their philosophy: cut the best deal, which means paying as little as possible. For them, there's nothing better than a young writer who's just tasted success. The flavor of the month. How naive can you get! He thinks he's lucid! He thinks he's cynical! He thinks he can discuss! I got on the phone and informed the magazine's editorial board that racial issues are very important to me.

"In what way?" the guy on the other end of the line asked.

"From the sexual point of view."

I don't know a single white who doesn't start salivating when the issue of interracial copulation is raised. As long as there's at least one taker, I'll have work in America.

"Why choose that point of view?"

12

The hypocrite!

"First of all, that's the only thing that interests me in North America."

"We're examining all the Americas, you understand. Central America, North America, South America and the Caribbean, too."

"Listen, whoever you are, I chose North America because I don't give a damn about the Mayans or the Aztecs. If you ask me, dead civilizations died because they didn't deserve to live."

"Since you come from the Caribbean, we thought that—"

"The same old garbage! People are supposed to write about where they came from! I write about what's going on around me, here and now, where I live."

"I wasn't implying that ..."

"Tell me what to write while you're at it!"

"It was only a suggestion."

"I won *my* American independence by banging at a typewriter eight hours a day. It was either that or the factory. I'll shoot the first guy who tries to take my Remington away from me, right between the eyes. I'm crazy, but I can shoot straight."

Okay, so I'm exaggerating, but only a little. It was just too much fun, pounding a nail into the soft, aristocratic skull of this overly polite young man who'd just stepped out of Harvard or one of those Ivy League schools that offers top-notch preparation to young Americans on how to starve the Third World from the comfort of Wall Street. Fortunately, they have no experience in hand-to-hand combat, which is how the hungry prefer to settle their accounts.

"That's fine, then," he stammered.

13

But I hadn't finished my explanations.

"What were the Aztecs, anyway? A bunch of degenerates, filthy rich, arrogant perverts, who made the people work for them. What is Aztec art? The work of guys on starvation wages. They've been replaced by the Americans who are no different. One day the whites will be replaced by the blacks. The blacks will be the worst imperialists the world's ever seen because they suffered so much. Never let people who've been through hell rule the world."

Total silence from the other end of the line. The enemy has been crushed. Now I can overrun the fortress. It's never been truer: war is raging in the New World.

IV

That's how I came to travel across North America. I watched the blacks and the whites and the reds and the yellows go about their business. I covered the waterfront. I can tell you this: everything they say about America is true. It integrates everything. The world's soft underbelly. The last innocent nation. Compared to them, the Bushmen are clever little devils. I know what you're saying. "Hold your horses, he's back with that old cliché about America the Innocent, that dead letter that perished years ago ..." I'm afraid not, brother, it's still in perfect working order. The machine is good as new. Two hundred years is just a wink of an eye in the history of humanity. America is an overfed infant. And Americans live as if no one else existed on the continent. On the planet. At the gas station where I fill up my car, I watch these magnificent barbarians at

14

play. Students from Indianapolis (according to their licence plate) playing football among the cars and gas pumps. They're wearing long T-shirts with their school colors. They're blond, tall and athletic. (Are you sure you're not laying it on a little thick? Sorry, brother, they really are like in our dreams.) Each of their movements seems absolutely new, as if they weren't connected to the human chain. They are unique. They devour tons of hamburgers, drink rivers of Coca-Cola and spend half their lives in front of a TV set. They pray to every god imaginable, and to one God, too. They kill with every possible method. They are strangers to remorse. The world is like a baby's rattle in their hands. They break it; they fix it. They know nothing about the past, and they despise the future. They are gods. And their blacks are demi-gods.

V

America demands only one thing: success. At any price, by any means. The word success has meaning only in America. What does it mean? That the gods love you. That human beings gather around you, breathe in your smell (the heady perfume of success), brush against you and, in the end, dance around you. You are a god. A god among the world's masters. You can't go any higher. This is the summit, the roof of the world. Here, you are looked upon. In America, he who looks is always the inferior one, until someone else shows up to look at him. The gaze is fast and furtive (fifteen seconds, not fifteen minutes, Warhol!); there's always something new to look at. The flavor of the month.

VI

For the longest time, writers despised success. You couldn't be both a good writer and a well-known writer. Writers were happy with their stingy print-runs, and they ended up at the mercy of publishers, booksellers and every possible go-between. Yet they thought they had the right to dole out moral instruction. The worst thing is how little it's all changed, even today. What young writer would dare turn down a contract for his first book with Knopf (just to give an example) because he didn't like the terms? Quite the opposite; he'd be happy to give the flesh of his flesh and the blood of his blood, five years of hard labor, for a few pennies. The day the contract is signed, he'll get together with a few friends to celebrate the occasion. Try and convince him, using the gentlest of terms, that Knopf is a business like any other (of course, of course) whose goal is to sell books, as many as possible. Try and tell him that this powerful company has an army of accountants and nervous heirs who spend more time paging through the spread sheets than reading the poems of Robert Lowell. Whisper those words in his ear and he'll squeal with horror. This young writer isn't writing to get rich or famous; he's writing to be read—and even that's a concession. I'm dumbstruck that such an intelligent, clear-sighted young man (at least that's what the critics say about him) can't seem to notice the extremely intimate relationship between being rich and famous, and being read. The more people read you, the more famous you'll be, and the more famous you are, the faster you'll get rich. Rich, and free. I, for one, have never lost sight of that equation.

16

How to Be Famous without Getting Tired

The title of my first novel made me famous. People who never read the book, especially those who had no intention of reading it, can quote you the title. It took me five minutes to come up with it. Three years to write the book. If only I'd known … Forget about those hundreds of scribbled pages; all I needed were ten little words: How to Make Love to a Negro without Getting Tired.

The different reactions to the title would make a case study in themselves.

1. A cocktail party in Outremont, a tony Montreal suburb.
"Are you the one who wrote the novel with that title?"
"I'm afraid so."
"Why do you say that? It's wonderful! You're so gifted!"
"Thank you."
(Should I make my move or not?)
She looked at me with a silly smile on her lips. Her husband smiled, too. They were art collectors who owned a clothing-store

chain.

"My husband hasn't read the book, but your title really made him laugh, I can tell you that." She laughed, too. "It's hilarious!"

"We sell lingerie in some of our stores in smaller cities." The man looked vaguely embarrassed. "I was telling my wife that your title would be great in our catalogue."

"Don't listen to him," his wife, a voluptuous redhead, interrupted. "All he thinks about is business."

"Not at all," I said. "I think it's a good idea."

She laughed noisily and clapped her hands, which seemed to be her nervous tic.

"You'd actually do it! That's great! And best of all, he's not pretentious! You know, I absolutely must see you again."

"Now, listen," the husband said, slipping into his hard-headed businessman's voice. "We'll try it out in the spring catalogue. If it works, we'll sign a contract. I'm not racist, you understand, but I have to wait and see how the clientele reacts. But don't worry, I'm almost sure it'll work."

"What are you talking about? Of course it'll work."

She smiled at me as if we were already accomplices.

"It'll be an honor for us to have your name in our catalogue."

The husband led his wife off to the bar.

"Don't forget, we absolutely have to see each other. I insist ..."

And she blew me a kiss.

2. In Madrid, a young feminist challenged me.

"I changed a word in your title. Do you want to know what it is?"

18

"Of course."

"How to make love to a Negro without getting *him* tired."

3. At the Leeds Film Festival, in England, this is what I told a girl who wanted to know why I chose a title like that.

"Young lady, if it weren't for that title, you probably wouldn't be here tonight."

The hall broke up.

4. In New York City, at the première of the film that was made from the novel, a girl (another one!) came up to me.

"Are you the author of that book?"

"Yes."

"Aren't you ashamed of using a title like that?"

"No."

She threw her glass of wine in my face.

5. In London, England, a very tall, very thin man put a drink into my hand.

"I've just finished a novel. My publisher tells me it will be a terrible success, but he doesn't like my title."

"Publishers are like that."

"My book is the first one, I believe," he said, smiling, "that speaks of a white man's attraction for black men."

"I see ..."

"According to my publisher, it's going to create a tremendous scandal. I have a favor to ask of you." His voice dropped. "It's very personal ... Naturally, you're free to say no."

Good Lord! I thought to myself, he's going to ask me to fellate him, right here, in the pub. These Englishmen are something else!

"May I borrow your title?"

"What?"

He smiled broadly.

"What do you think? It's never been done before—at least, never with the author's permission. My publisher says that if you agree, it's legally feasible. Your title is the only one that fits my subject. I've racked my brains, believe me, but all I find is your title."

"If mine is the only one, then take it. But I'm warning you, it'll bring you misery. It's not the kind of title you can get rid of easily."

"*How to Make Love to a Negro without Getting Tired*, by John Ferguson. My publisher will be absolutely overjoyed. You know, my publisher is a personal friend of Salman Rushdie's."

6. In Paris, a young woman who saw the lighter side of life told me over a glass of wine at the Café de Flore, "I bought your book, you know, but not to read it. I put it on my bedside table; it scares off pretenders."

7. A young white man in Chicago found the title offensive. A young black man in Los Angeles found it racist. A young Montreal woman found it sexist. *Jackpot!*

8. In Toronto, a woman was reading the book in a bus when she noticed that everyone was looking at her strangely.

"I didn't realize that people could read the title on the cover."

"And?"

20

"I've never been so embarrassed in my life."

9. In Tokyo, the title was completely changed because, as the Japanese distributor told me, "We don't have words like that in Japanese."

10. In Rome, a thin woman, just skin and bones, heading towards sixty, the contessa type, whispered in my ear.

"You'll never guess where I tattooed your title ..."

"I give up."

"That's what I thought," she said mysteriously, then slipped into the crowd of party-goers at the Duchessa Bocconcini's villa.

How the hell could she have put a title that long on such a small body?

11. In Port-au-Prince, a very demanding friend told me, "The title's the only good thing about your book."

12. In Brussels, an African writer practically screamed at me, "Mark my words, brother, in three weeks no one will even remember your book!"

13. In Antwerp, the translator improved on the title which became, in Dutch, *How to Make Love to a Negro without Turning Black.*

14. In the United States, all the major daily papers censored the title. The *New York Times,* the *Washington Post,* the *Miami Herald,* the *Los Angeles Times,* the *Chicago Tribune,* the *Daily News*, the *Boston Globe*, the *New York Post*. Every last one.

I was asked to change the title. I told them it was up to America to change.

15. In San Francisco, everyone liked the title. But that's San Francisco.

16. In Sydney, Australia, a straightforward young woman challenged me to prove the veracity of my title.

There are days like that.

17. In Stockholm, a young blonde (what a coincidence!) introduced me to her black lover.

"Ask Seko," she laughed, "who gets tired first."

"Seko, no doubt," I said.

Seko laughed a giant Guinean laugh.

"How to make love to two Negroes without getting tired," she murmured with night in her eyes.

Seko stopped laughing.

18. In Amsterdam, a young white South African woman demanded an answer to this painful question.

"How *do* you make love to a Negro without getting tired?"

"Let him do all the work."

19. All around the world, everyone asks me the same question. Why did you choose that title? Well, why not? One thing's for sure: I never want to hear about it again. I've overdosed on it. Nowadays, it makes me sick.

I'm going to tell you how it got started, once and for all. Bouba thought it up. I remember, we were walking down the rue Saint-Denis, in Montreal. It was raining. A summer rain. And Bouba said, as if in a dream, very slowly, "How to make love to a Negro when it's raining and you have nothing better to do." His title was too long, but it was funnier.

My first novel. The gods could at least have waited for the third before hitting on me. The first shot. Bull's-eye. Not even the first novel. The first novel's *title*.

Landscapes

Sex doesn't cause AIDS; disgust with sex does. The
Western world's disgust. Who has to pay the piper
now? The Third World, as usual. People don't understand that sex is the only productive leisure activity
that the poor have. The Third World exists in North
America, too. The ghettos full of a teeming black
population, poor, illiterate, where teenage mothers
mix crack and powdered milk. The child will be born
blind, drug-dependent, sick. But that legacy won't kill
him; death will come from a bullet to the head at the
corner of 125th and Broadway.

—Notebook 13

I filled eighteen notebooks with field notes and took hundreds
of photos. America is a succession of snapshots. The structure
of American cities guided my article. Big cities aren't linked
with a view to forming a group or nation. They are scattered
through the landscape, each with its personality, independence, mood, style—but all are obsessed with the driving

desire to be American cities. The smaller towns are rat-holes with the same stores, the same banks, the same half-dozen McDonald's and other fast-food restaurants, the same pig-faced policemen who live for Saturday night, the same corrupt daily paper and the same dullard teenagers. What is an American city? American reality (space, time, people and objects) is more cinema than novel, more jump cut than dissolve, scenes that run over each other and don't follow any logical sequence, more rage than courage, more instinct than mind. If American reality is a feature film, than the life of an average American is a video.

That's why American writers (and here I'm not talking about the manufacturers of bestsellers that lie in heaps by the supermarket check-out) have so many problems with the novel and seem to do much better with the short story. In general, the contemporary American novel is a collection of short texts strung together on a solid but flexible chain: the sense of being American. The American way of life is a collection of facts (the sensation of nothingness). This book is no exception.

PART ONE

Where?

I Am a Black Writer

A girl came up to me in the street.

"Are you the writer?"

"Sometimes."

"Can I ask you a question?"

"Of course."

"Is the book *your* story?"

"What do you mean by that?"

"I saw you on TV the other day, and I was wondering whether all those things really happened to you."

"Yes and no."

She wasn't surprised or confused; she just wanted a straight explanation.

"Is that it?"

"I don't know what to tell you ... No one can tell a story exactly the way it happened. You fix it up. You try to find the key emotion. You fall into the trap of nostalgia. And there's nothing further from the truth than nostalgia."

"So it really isn't your story."

"May I ask *you* a question?"

"Why would you do that?" she blushed. "I never wrote a book."

"But you read books."

"I like to read."

"Why is it so important to know if the story really happened to the author?"

She thought about that one.

"You just want to know."

"I see ... Why?"

"I don't know," she said with a pained smile. "You feel closer to him that way."

"What if he was lying to you?"

"What do you mean?"

"What if he told you it was his story, even if it really wasn't?"

"I'd be disappointed," she laughed, a little embarrassed. "I suppose we never know the truth."

"So why bother?"

"It's just a fantasy."

She laughed.

"Are you keeping something from me?"

"Maybe, but I don't know what."

She smiled again.

"Where do you like to read?" I asked her.

"Anywhere."

"In the subway?"

"There, too."

Nothing fascinates me more than a girl reading in the subway. I don't know why, but Tolstoy wins it hands down underground. With *Anna Karenina,* naturally.

"Some people read anywhere, but not just anything," I

said, without really knowing what that meant.

She gave me a penetrating look.

"I read anything."

"Which means you're the perfect reader."

A car swept by. She leapt aside to safety.

"I'm sure you don't finish every book."

"Sorry, I didn't catch that," she said, getting over her fright.

"When you start a book, do you always finish it?"

"Always."

By now, she had recovered her wits.

"There's something here that doesn't add up," I told her.

"Maybe because I never remember anything," she chuckled.

"How can that be?"

"I don't remember the author's name ..."

My heart sank.

"... Or even the title of the book."

"I suppose that really isn't important. The book's the only thing that matters."

She sighed.

"I never remember the subject either. Sometimes I think I've never read a single book in my life."

"That's incredible! You read something, and a minute later it's gone?"

"I'm afraid so."

A long pause.

"Then why read?"

"It passes the time."

"I see ... Does it bother you when you forget?"

"Oh, yes!"

She seemed hurt that I would ask her such a question.

"I imagine your forgetfulness causes trouble in the rest of your life."

"No. It only happens with books. Do you think I'm disturbed? Sorry—not at all. I work in an office not far from here, and believe it or not, you need a good memory in my line of work. I'm a legal secretary."

"Why did you come up to me in the street? You seem like the shy type to me."

A peal of fine laughter burst from her throat.

"I am shy, you're right. I don't know why. I guess because I saw you on TV."

"Maybe you've read one of my books ..."

"No. At least, I don't think so."

A moment's hesitation.

"Well, maybe yes. I might have read one of your books."

"There's no way of being vain around you."

She laughed her shy laugh.

"I'm sorry."

"I'd like to ask you something."

"Yes," she breathed, turning her head to one side.

"Are you in love?"

This time, her laughter was harsh.

"You're a strange one ... But why not, you're a writer."

"A black writer," I pointed out.

"What's that mean? Is it better?"

"Unfortunately, not."

"So?"

"That's the way it is."

"Is it?"

"Yes."

32

"Too bad."

"There are certain advantages, you know."

"For example?"

"There are fewer of us. It's easier to become the greatest living black writer."

"Then what?" she asked slyly.

"Then you die, of course."

My eye was briefly captured by a girl walking on the other side of the street. A girl with an enormously short green skirt, a veritable handkerchief, and legs that must be worth more than a brooch from Tiffany's. When I turned back to continue the conversation, the reader had gone. Where did she come from? Where was she going? What did she want from me? No sense asking those questions in America.

America, We Are Here

Back then, I was trying to write a book and survive in America at the same time. (I'll never figure out how that ambition wormed its way into me.) One of those two pursuits had to go. Time to choose, man. But a problem arose: I wanted everything. That's the way drowning men are. I wanted a novel, girls (fascinating girls, the products of modernity, weight-loss diets, the mad longings of older men), alcohol and laughter. My due—that's all. That which America had promised me. I know America has made a lot of promises to a very large number of people, but I was intent on making her keep her word. I was furious at her, and I don't like to be double-crossed. At the time, I'm sure you'll remember, at the beginning of the 1980s (so long ago!), the bars in any North American city were chock-full of confused, aging hippies—they were confused before they became hippies—empty-eyed Africans who always had a drum within easy striking distance—the type never changes, no matter the location or the decade—Caribbeans in search of their identity, starving white poetesses who lived off alfalfa sprouts and Hindu mythology, aggressive

34

young black girls who knew they didn't stand a chance in this insane game of roulette because the black men were only into white women, and the white guys into money and power. Late in the evening, I wandered through these lunar landscapes where sensations had long since replaced sentiment. I took notes. I scribbled away in the washrooms of crummy bars. I carried on endless conversations until dawn with starving intellectuals, out-of-work actresses, philosophers without influence, tubercular poetesses, the bottomest of the bottom dogs. I jumped into that pool once in a while and found myself in a strange bed with a girl I didn't remember having courted (I left the bar last night with the black-haired girl, I'm sure I did, so what's this bottle-blonde with the green fingernails doing here?). But I never took drugs. God had given me the gift of loud, powerful, happy, contagious laughter, a child's laugh that drove girls wild. They wanted to laugh so badly, and there wasn't much to laugh about back then. When I immigrated to North America, I made sure I brought that laughter in my battered metal suitcase, an ancestral legacy. We always laughed a lot around my house. My grandfather's deep laughter would shake the walls. I laughed, I drank wine, I made love with the energy of a child who's been locked inside a candy shop, and I wrote it all down. As soon as the girl scampered off to the bathroom, I would start scribbling down notes. The edge of a bed or the corner of a table was my desk. I'd note down a good line, a sensual walk, a pained smile, all the details of life. Everything fascinated me. I wrote down everything that moved, and things never stopped moving, believe me. All around me, the world (the girl, the dress on the floor, my underwear lost in the sheets, that long naked back moving towards the stereo, then Bob Marley's music), the elements of my universe turned at top speed. How could words halt the flight of time, girls wheeling away, desire burning anew? Often I would fall asleep with my head against my old Remington, asking myself those unanswerable questions. Am I the troubadour of low-rent America, always on the edge of an overdose, up against the wall, handcuffs slapped on, with two cops breathing down my neck? America discounting her life, counting her pennies, the America of immigrants, blacks and poor white girls who've lost their way? America of empty eyes and pallid dawn. In the end, I wrote that damned novel, and America was forced, at least as far as I was concerned, to come through on a few of her promises. I know she gives more to some than they need; with others, she swipes the hunk of stale bread from their clenched fists. But I made her pay at least a third of her debt. I'm naive, I know, I can see the audience smiling, but my mental system needs to believe in this victory, as tiny as it may be. A third of a victory. For others, not a penny of the debt has been paid. America owes an enormous amount to Third World youth. I'm not just talking about historical debt (slavery, the rape of natural resources, the balance of payments, etc.); there's a sexual debt, too. Everything we've been promised by magazines, posters, the movies, television. America is a happy hunting ground, that's what gets beaten into our heads every day, come and stalk the most delicious morsels (young American beauties with long legs, pink mouths, superior smiles), come and pick the wild fruit of this new Promised Land. For you, young men of the Third World, America will be a doe quivering under the buckshot of your caresses. The call went out around the world, and we heard it,

36

even the blue men of the desert heard it. Remember the global village? They've got American TV in the middle of the Sahara. Westward, ho! It was a new gold-rush. And when each new arrival showed up, he was told, "Sorry, the party's over." I can still picture the sad smile of that Bedouin, old in years but still vigorous (remember, brother, those horny old goats from the Old Testament), who had sold his camel to attend the party. I met up with all of them in a tiny bar on Park Avenue. While you're waiting for the next fiesta, the manpower counselor told us, you have to work. There's work for everyone in America (the old carrot and stick, brother). We've got you coming and going. What? Work? Our Bedouin didn't come here to work. He crossed the desert and sailed the seas because he'd been told that in America the girls were free and easy. Oh, no, you didn't quite understand! What didn't we understand? All the songs and novels and films from America ever since the end of the 1950s talk about sex and sex alone, and now you're telling us we didn't understand? Didn't understand what? What were we supposed to have understood from that showy sexuality, that profusion of naked bodies, that total disclosure, that Hollywood heat? You should know we have some very sophisticated devices in the desert; we can tune in America. The resolution is exceptional, and there's no interference in the Sahara. In the evening, we gather in our tents lit by the cathode screen and watch you. Watching how you do what you do is a great pleasure for us. Some pretty girl is always laughing on a beach somewhere. The next minute, a big blond guy shows up and jumps her. She slips between his fingers, and he chases her into the surf. She fights, but he holds her tight and both of them sink to the bottom. Every evening it's the same

37

menu, with slight variations. The sea is bluer, the girl blonder, the guy more muscled. All our dreams revolve around this life of ease. That's what we want: the easy life. Those breasts and asses and teeth and laughter—after a while, it started affecting our libido. What could be more natural? And now, here we are in America, and you dare tell us that we didn't understand? Understand what? I ask the question again. What were we supposed to have understood? You made us mad with desire. Today, we stand before you, a long chain of men (in our country, adventure is the realm of men), penises erect, appetites insatiable, ready for the battle of the sexes and the races. We'll fight to the finish, America.

The Tree of America

I didn't even go there to drink. I just wanted to see what that Park Avenue bar had become. The one where I used to hang out during the darkest period of my life, when I kept sinking and wondering whether I'd ever hit bottom. When you drown, man, you have to be ready to swallow a little water. I could drink the whole river before I found someone to throw me a life preserver. I could hear their laughter, their games, their love-making. The bright voices of the girls, the virile shouts of the men, the sensual tones of the women. A river bottom has marvelous acoustics; you can hear everything the living are doing up above. The music of life. The song of the plants, the air, the wind. Even fetuses can't turn down the invitation. They leave the world of water for the mortal world of air. I would sleep twelve or eighteen hours a day, and spend the rest of the time watching television. I couldn't pull myself away from those game shows. I could tell you the price of every household detergent on the market. I knew the price of what America was selling, down to the last cent. And the price was right. I swallowed it all. The most fantastic propaganda machine human beings have ever devised. America, forever clamoring that life is a party and that the trees of the Promised Land are heavy with wild, full, succulent fruit. Unfortunately, the tree of America also produces some bitter fruit, too. You have to climb the ladder of Judeo-Christian society to get the sweet fruit; the other kind is always close at hand.

No Return Allowed Beyond This Limit

A dark, smoky bar. Reggae music. Marley. The wretched of
the earth. Indians, South Americans, Asians, blacks. Only the
women are white. The maximum number of colors. The stage
is hardly as big as two ping-pong tables. The sound of bodies
brushing together like fabric rent asunder. Cosmopolitan
odors. Heavy desire. Cannibalism is the absolute manifesta-
tion of tenderness. Love at its essential degree. I'll eat you up.
Promises! Okay, I warned you. The taste of a woman. Her
sweat makes it salty. Salsa. Bodies melded together. Dry
mouths. Dreaming of tropical rain. Right here, in a Park
Avenue bar. Nothing's changed since my time. I could come
back in fifty years and see the same scene. The laws of attraction don't vary in the world of the night. The oldest ritual. You
show up, you climb the steep stairs, you drop off your coat at
the coat check (don't forget the tip, brother, if you intend to
come back), you sit down, watch, a waitress appears, you give
her a look of disbelief, and she slinks away a little shamefully,
you say hi to your friends, the waitress comes back, you pretend not to see her, and you go find another table. A girl is

shaking it out on the floor. Not bad. You get the low-down. She's new. You try your luck. It's okay with her. You dance. Merengue. Salsa. Reggae. She doesn't want to any more. You head for greener pastures. Maybe a piss. You meet a guy in the washroom. You talk a little. You come out and run right into the waitress. You order a beer, then you spot (like a flame wavering at the end of a tunnel) a girl you know conversing with a guy you hate, but luckily he splits, you go over to the girl, what a smile she has, as if she's been waiting for you all her life. The waitress taps you on the shoulder. You pay for the beer, take a little sip, then ask the girl to dance. You move against her cool skin. Zaire music. Sensual rhythms. Hot and cool. Everything is going according to plan. The usual routine!

For the Sake of the Trade

Here's where it all happens: war, life, death, lovesickness, VD, violence, brutal break-ups, fatal attractions. Here, on this tiny plot of ground. Shows nightly, at this time (eleven at night till three in the morning) and place (the dance floor). With the same characters (Jenny, Charlie, Adam, Cham and me, back then). Pull up a chair (as I'm doing now) and watch the great show of our times as it plays out. Races, sexes, classes, religions, everything thrown together for the purpose of our entertainment. Humankind has devised perverse games and practices meaningless rituals. Entertaining us is surely what Jenny has in mind when, every night, she throws a jealous tantrum, locks herself up in the bathroom and tells us she's going to slit her wrists. Entertainment is certainly Cham's objective when he manages to get his girlfriend stolen by Charlie, before getting beaten up by the same Charlie because he tried to take her back while Charlie was off shooting up. Sheer entertainment when Jenny and Charlie's new girlfriend (Cham's ex) start flailing away at each other in the stairway while Charlie laughs himself silly from the top step. Come

43

back in fifty years; you'll see the same show. It's like Mass: the offertory when Charlie lays eyes on Cham's girl, the gospel when he starts his dumb-ass little rap about how blondes absolutely have to have black flesh and the consecration when the girl walks by, practically screaming, "Here is my body, eat it; here is my blood, drink it!" Charlie takes her into the men's john, and no one can take a piss for the next couple of hours. Sometimes three. Ite missa est. Why does the biggest asshole always win? I'll tell you: because he's not just any asshole, he's the biggest one. Bigness is what works in America. Find a niche, any niche, and be the best at it. It's that simple. Let's take an example. You're a writer, right? Well, kind of … You're a writer, yes or no? You've got to know what you are; this ain't Europe or something. Are you a writer? Yes, I think so. Okay, that's better. You know, man, in this life, you've got to make up your mind. Imagine if you asked a plumber the same question. Are you a plumber? Well, kind of … You wouldn't let him touch your pipes with an answer like that.

I was lost in thoughts of this magnitude when I felt a powerful arm go around my neck.

"Hey, if it ain't our star!"

I knew who it was.

"Hello, Charlie."

He went on squeezing my neck.

"Hey, man."

I started gasping for breath.

"To what do we owe the honor, man?"

"I just stopped by for a drink, Charlie."

Charlie kept on squeezing.

"What do you mean, you just stopped by for a drink?"

44

"Just what it sounds like, Charlie."

I was having difficulty speaking.

"How about your old friends, don't they count any more?"

"Of course they count, Charlie."

"Yeah? That's not the way it looks."

He pushed me, and I knocked over the table. It fell on the foot of some girl wearing a ton of necklaces. She screamed.

"Shit, Charlie, cut the crap! I just came here to have a quiet drink."

Charlie went for my throat again.

"You told me that already."

We hit the floor, and I cut my arm on a broken bottle-neck. My blood stained Charlie's shirt, and Charlie thought he was hurt. Finally I got away from him and went into the washroom. My left arm was covered in blood, but it was really only a scratch. I don't know why Charlie thinks I put him in my novel. All right, I did steal a few of his features for one of my characters, but the character wasn't just him. Of course, Charlie and Adam were both writing novels back then (by the way, whatever happened to those works of genius?), and Cham, too, and even me (one-third of the time). I represent one-third of that damned novel. *And I wrote it, too.* But Charlie could never understand that. He thinks I just observed him and wrote the book. True, I did transcribe a few of his ripostes. He's the one who once said to a girl he just dropped, "Times are tough for everybody, baby." Everyone in the bar knows I owe that one to Charlie, but that's what all writers do, if you ask me. They eat people up and shit out words. I bet Charlie never even read the book. That's his pride and joy: he never read a single book in his life. Okay, but why is everybody else looking at me that

45

way? Naiveté strikes again: I thought I'd receive a hero's welcome. Blacks have been all the rage ever since my book came out. They've never been so popular. Finally, someone's talking about us the way we want to be talked about. I figured the blacks were going to honor me with pomp and circumstance and say, "Check out that guy who beat the whites at their own game. Sure, we've been musicians and athletes, but words have held out on us so far, and now this clever mother comes along and cuts his way right into the heart of the alphabet. And what's better, he comes back to our side, in one piece, to the cheers of the white liberal crowd. All we hope is that he made lots of good white money. That's because the yuppies and old squaws go for his trash. We blacks don't need a book that's going to tell us how to screw better because we picked it up at our mama's breast. We're not going to spend a single cent on this grade-one book that tells how a clever black man made his way through the jungle. We'll wish him luck, that's all." That's the kind of palaver under the baobab tree I was expecting; I was totally mistaken. I remember when Cham and I used to be poor, gifted and black, thinking about how we were going to change the world so we could get a bigger slice of the pie. We used to say that books about blacks were always too nice and too cautious, and since they were smeared with the vaseline of Judeo-Christian guilt, they'd never get to the heart of the matter; in other words, they were lousy, lousy, lousy, lousy, lousy, lousy. When a black writes one, it's even worse. The same old crap, "In Praise of the Race" or something like that. And that, man, Cham would tell me in his reed-like voice, has nothing to do with literature, nothing! Literature means sweeping aside the veils, nothing more, nothing less. Revealing what you're

46

supposed to hide. Anyway, that's what Cham and I used to say back when Lady Luck wasn't smiling on us. We had our little discussions (very highfalutin, you know the type) until the evening someone (a girl, Jenny, I think) announced that Adam was writing a book and that she'd read a chapter of it and that it was absolute dynamite. No one believed for one second that Adam could write an explosive book, let alone read one. The girl (maybe it wasn't Jenny) let on that we were completely wrong about Adam, that she knew a little about men and that Adam was exactly the kind of guy who would turn out to be a serial killer. A frustrated dreamer. Silence settled upon the table (that's right, it was at Jenny's place, but I can't remember who was doing the talking). In her opinion, Adam was the prototypical writer. A perverse being pulling frayed and rotten strings. An impotent type. A voyeur. A dreamer of small dreams. *Voilà,* that's a writer for you. It was like a kick in the gut. Writers, you say? Impotent stool-pigeons ready to sell themselves when they run out of friends to sell. They should be held accountable for the murders and other humiliations to which they cynically subject their characters, the rumors they traffic in, the old clichés they dust off. Instead, readers have turned them into cowardly, weak and irresponsible creatures by encouraging their treacherous gossip. Perhaps, unconsciously, that's why I returned to the scene to be judged by those who had become the characters of my imaginary world after having first been my friends. Which is why I let myself be pushed around by Charlie. For the sake of the trade.

47

The Carl Lewis of the Typewriter

I didn't know it was going to be so hard. I saw them off in the distance, on the mountain-top, where the air is clear. Cool, too. Regular gods! I envied them with all my heart and soul. I had to make my way to the top, no matter what. There where the fruit tastes sweet, where the vegetables are greener (I got that from Truman Capote, who spent a lifetime frequenting the rich), where the girls are all nymphets (any dribbling old fossil with a bank account in the six figures will tell you that), where all is for the best in this, the best of worlds. Leave the rest of them far below, stewing in their stinking juices. I abjure regret and nostalgia, for poverty was never very nice to me. If some people are up there, that must mean it's feasible. And if it's feasible, why not me? But first you have to understand this: to accede to the top, you have to become very light, very, very light. You have to float, man. Drop everything heavy: worries, false problems (and, especially, true ones), adolescent dreams, regrets, everything that grabs onto you by the ankles and keeps you from climbing lightly up the ladder of Judeo-Christian society. When you get there, you've got to be in excellent

48

shape, like a professional athlete. The Carl Lewis of the type-writer. Slender, supple, nerves of steel, burning with ambition. Be the fastest writer alive, if you can't be the best. A book in under ten seconds. Now there's a challenge, man. You've got to slave away at it (pardon the expression) with a stopwatch in one hand, like any champion. All the trades are trying to adjust to these fast-paced times of ours. Writers are the only ones not listening. Then they act surprised as rock musicians and hockey players streak by them on their way up the hit parade. Even journalism has gotten into step. But writers go on spinning their outdated plots without any thought for the present. They're bringing up the rear, followed only by sculptors. We should have been the first to figure it out because, so it's said, writing is an attempt to gain mastery over time. Mastering time—what a joke! Time has come to a standstill on our sheets of white paper. Dead time. Real time keeps on running. Look at the athletes outside your window. There they are, self-confident, alive, living at fever pitch, their left eye never leaving the stopwatch's face. They know what they want and what they're worth, down to a tenth of a second. Have you ever seen Carl Lewis' demeanor? That's the kind of look I want. Lewis is the kind of man who's used to putting himself on the line to find out exactly what he's worth. Stopwatch in hand, he doesn't have time to worry about the state of his soul. He does it as often as you go to the laundromat. Meanwhile, writers go wandering through their artistic fog. Sometimes it makes me sick. Too few writers can point to their exact spot on the flow chart. Theirs is one of the last trades to systematically practice modesty, that virtuous form of hypocrisy. And to think that we write as an act of self-discovery. Of course, we could always say—and we'd be right—that Carl Lewis and Hemingway don't practice the same trade. Though I don't think Hemingway would have agreed. He always wanted to bring sports and writing closer together. It was a good try, too. Especially since, at the time, athletes hardly earned anything. Today, Carl Lewis can make millions for less than ten seconds of work. Now, there's a job that's moved ahead by leaps and bounds! Why do people still think that the expenditure of brain energy is superior to muscle energy? What makes us think that a writer is more intelligent than an athlete? One of them uses his brain, you say? Sure, but which one? The man or woman who spends three years on a novel that'll bring in five thousand bucks at the very most, or Carl Lewis? Of course, but ... But what? Being a writer is more prestigious than being an athlete? Go ahead, believe it if it helps you to keep on writing, brother.

A Black Writer Thinks Best
in the Dark

You'll need a good pair of lungs, man. But once you cross
through the ozone layer and ease into another space, you won't
have to worry any more. Things will work out all by themselves. They'll come to you of their own accord, without you
having to take the trouble to desire them. But before you reach
that height, you've got to work your butt off! The knot is
pulled so tight you wonder whether you'll ever be able to untie
it. That's when you'll have to be patient and, thread by thread,
take it apart. Even when it's over it won't be over. You'll come
to an even more complicated knot, and you'll need even more
patience and, of course, before you untie them all, you'll be
seventy years old and have the right to say you've been
screwed over. So delete everything I just said. Let's start all
over again, brother. Just stop thinking about it, and it'll happen
naturally, like an uninterrupted orgasm. Paradise, right? You
wake up one morning and start typing like crazy, and pretty
soon you'll have that short novel the whole world's been pant-
ing after. You tell yourself, "This can't be real, it can't be this

easy, something must be wrong with me. I don't feel completely myself. Who's that little devil playing tricks on me?" But you keep on typing, your fingers are on fire. You're not hungry or thirsty, you don't even feel like sex. You're on another level, and you're sure that if you stop, you'll never start again, so you keep on. You're not too sure you know what you're writing, but you know it's way bigger than you are, and that there's someone else in the room, just behind you. You feel Old Scratch's breath on the back of your neck. In the end, your head drops, and you begin speaking in tongues. You're possessed, man. Old Scratch has got your soul. Unfortunately, this kind of thing never happens in real life. In my life, in any case. Well, man, I hate to say it but you're mistaken, it's happened before. Who to? Take a look around. No, not out the window, look on your bookshelves. That's right. *The Little Prince.* Fifty-odd pages of typescript, and you're eternal, it's that simple. Just to bug the American bestseller machine with its 600-page bricks. I'm talking about 600 typed pages, single spaced. Every page stuffed with detailed information about the characters (what they eat, drink, the clothes they wear, their daily routines, the name of the bar where they go drinking, the name of the drink, the cocktail recipe, etc.). At that rate, you can lay down 600 pages in a month's time. Why not ten thousand, for that matter? The more the better. Cover the surface of the earth. These people have nothing to say, and they need three volumes to say it in. What about the public? The public, friend, is impressed by the sheer volume (ten pounds easily), and it buys these shrink-wrapped packs of tasteless bulk without concern for quality. "Give me two more, Ma'am, plus the big one that's hiding behind Michener, no, no, not Stephen King, I can't take him. I heard that little green men write his books, his ghost-writers come from Mars. I read that in the *Enquirer*, and if he does write his own books, I think he writes too many, I don't like that, he writes so fast that every time I begin one, another one has already come out. Do you consider that normal? I think I'll take another Irving. I love bears, and I hope there'll be some in it … All right, that's enough for today, the long weekend's coming up, and I'm taking everyone to Disneyworld." Guys like Irving, Michener and King (I'm leaving out the ones who are both unreadable and unknown) come from all the top American universities. They're used to working hard, taking copious notes, penning voluminous memoirs, and that's probably the way they dress and dance and make love. Their faith … Their perseverance … They're in it for the long haul … So start hauling ass … Blacken those reams of paper with meaningless words. A story with no perspective. Meanwhile, *The Little Prince* is there, slender and straight on the shelf, patiently waiting for the centuries to come and sit at its feet like a wise child. Creating something like that is such sweet revenge against those polluters, something as soft and round and pure as Saint-Exupéry's masterpiece—then go out and buy yourself a Jaguar with the money it brings in. If the Holy Spirit exists, now's the time for him to step forward; it's his last chance.

Why have I worked myself into this state? What else can I do, lying here in darkness with the window open onto the immense American sky?

53

Turning through the South

I got on a Greyhound bus yesterday evening. We drove all night. I read a little, then slept some. The bus finally stopped in a small southern town that had the name of a European capital (Rome, Paris or Berlin).

I peered out the window. The gas station lit up a wide perimeter with harsh, colorless light. A dog howled somewhere in the night. I'd often seen this kind of tableau in bad German expressionist films. We must be in Berlin, USA. The door to the bus flew open. The driver worked it with a lever by the wheel. Everyone made a beeline for the exit to get out and stretch their legs. I kept my seat, paging through Naipaul's *A Turn in the South,* a book I've been carrying with me for some time. Naipaul inspires ambivalence in me. On the one hand he's a master of calm, solid, well-balanced prose, with a sting of irony that lurks between the lines of his narration. At the same time, I'm often overcome by the fumes of boredom that his purposely heavy sentences give off. Sometimes, you need a mask to read Naipaul.

A half hour later, they came streaming back, their bodies a bit more refreshed, their conversation and pace a bit more lively. The herd returning to the barn. The driver took on a dozen more passengers, whom he seated wherever he could, creating a gentle kind of chaos in this opaque night. Besides the outrageously lit gas station, everything was as black as India ink. I could scarcely make out a few dimly lit houses. Here, people sleep with their televisions on. The driver showed a girl to the empty seat next to me, then gave me a wink as he went back to the wheel. The girl stowed her bag under her seat. I watched her go about her business. She smiled at me as she took a book out of her purse. One of those bestsellers I'm allergic to. Judging by the cover illustration, it's one of those Southern stories again. When you've read *Gone with the Wind,* you've read them all. I took out my notebook and began scribbling down a few lines. The bus, at night. The South. I think of Styron who, to a certain extent, defended America's South, with all its terrors. Styron is an honest man and an admirable writer. I respect his anguish. I thought of Faulkner, too. Faulkner dreaming of the slaves on his family farm. Back in those happy days of slavery in the Old South. Poor Faulkner could not free himself from that era. Negroes sweating in the cotton fields. I picture Baldwin's anger and comprehend it. Baldwin vs. Faulkner. Faulkner who wanted the Negroes to be patient just a little longer so they wouldn't upset the South's fragile psychology. Meanwhile, Baldwin sensed that the whole thing was going to blow up in America's insouciant face. Faulkner vs. Baldwin. The great Southern writer, Nobel Prize winner, the gentleman farmer with his rustic manners facing off against the skinny genius of Harlem. Faulkner is a vast writer who could never get inside the skin of a Southern black. He was blind to the great scandal of slavery; blind, deaf and

55

dumb. The great teller of America's story. We all have our limits. Baldwin is the young prophet announcing the apocalypse: the fire next time. How do I feel sitting next to a Southern girl? Calm down, now, this isn't South Africa. I hate those people who lose all perspective at the slightest hint of a racist act, who conjure up Hitler for every small-time demagogue. Moderation, brother. She turned to me and asked if I wouldn't mind giving her my window seat because she's a little claustrophobic. What am I to make of a girl so fragile? Only Southern blacks know something about that. Here's a kindly girl, a little disturbed, who must have friendly parents, attentive friends, warm-hearted neighbors in the Southern tradition. They all go to church on Sunday, work hard for charity and do volunteer work for a hospital, an old folks' home or an orphanage. I believe the South is bursting with saintly people. Then what's wrong with this picture? How can these same people also be part of the Ku Klux Klan and ostentatiously forget to celebrate Martin Luther King's birthday, fight integration in the schools (it wasn't so long ago, brother) and head for the hills whenever an upstanding black family wants to move into the neighborhood? History explains everything, of course. Many small individual stories that, like streams, pour into the great river. Most Southerners are far from being racist, whereas the South itself remains violently racist. What can we do with such information? A racist country in which no one is racist is a mystery to me. It's all but impossible for me to consider a Southerner the same way as anyone else. Each time, history marches before my eyes. I find the process exhausting. What good are such thoughts? My boiling blood won't help solve anything. I dozed off. I can sleep, even dream, under any

56

condition. It's a gift, brother. I woke up when the bus stopped in another little town exactly like the one before and probably like the one after. The same crowd pushed out of the bus, gasping for clean air. Another violently lit gas station. It's like the structure of a nightmare; Miller's air-conditioned one. I, for one, won't leave my seat. Small American towns give me indigestion. I can't help but ask the same stupid question: why is it that people choose to live in dumps like this? Strange, but I never ask that question in Africa or South America. These small American towns are odorless, colorless, disinfected— except for the germ of stupidity. I take them as a personal affront, as if they were telling me, "You're leaving in fifteen minutes, and I know you'll never come back." How right they are! And that's what breaks my heart: in America, all I see are the big cities. I can't accept people who are without the slightest grain of ambition. What the Harvard intellectuals call America makes me sick to my stomach. Erskine Caldwell is the only one who could find it charming. My seat-mate got out with the other passengers. A moment later, the bus was empty. She was modestly dressed, but an expert eye (like mine, brother) could easily distinguish her body under her floral-print dress. A body accustomed to strict regimentation. The body of a young WASP consumed by the worst parasite: sexual hypocrisy. I pictured her singing in the integrated choir, and spontaneously my penis began to rise. The crowd returned. A scant ten minutes to stretch your legs and strike up a completely meaningless conversation with a stranger. The passengers settled in; her seat was empty. The bus barreled through the night to the next crummy little town. I picked up Naipaul's book and fell asleep after a dozen sentences.

57

PART TWO

Why?

Why Must a Black Writer Always Have a Political Opinion?

First of all, must a black writer have a color? That's the kind of question I have to face, wherever I go. In the subway, at a restaurant (he eats, too, the bastard!), on my way to the park to see a game, in a taxi.

The taxi driver is Nigerian. He told me right away. He hadn't been back to his country for twenty years. Actually, I'm African, he went on—as if I couldn't tell. He was referring to his color, which wasn't black, but dark blue, with scarification on his cheeks and behind his ears. He explained to me that the colonizers cut up Africa into its present shape. He was against it, naturally. He admits to being Nigerian only because people are forever asking him where he's from. People are so dense. At first, he held out, explaining that there is only one race in Africa and that the expression "black Africa" is not only a pleonasm, but a political stupidity, an infamy, one more piece of garbage invented by the West to cast doubt in the minds of Africans. Color does not exist in Africa. When everyone is the same color, color ceases to be a factor; epidermal differences disappear. What about South Africa? He didn't want to talk about it, the subject gets him too upset. South Africa makes him see red: a black seeing red. He laughed heartily at his own pun. Once he picked up a fare and it turned out that the guy was pro-apartheid. He turned around and punched him in the face. The guy pressed charges and he spent a month on unemployment. He wasn't sorry. The judge told him that here in America we have democracy, and everybody has the right to his opinion. He yelled at the judge that the guy was a racist bastard and started hollering his head off in the courtroom until they threw him out with a month in jail and the promise that, next time, they would take away his licence. His lawyer tried to tell him that if he hadn't made such a stink, he would have gotten off with a week. He wasn't sorry about that either, but now he's careful not to bring up the subject with customers. But if a guy gets in his car and makes a racist remark, there's no telling what he might do. If you lose your job, you can always find another one. But if you lose your dignity, you lose everything. "And you can't buy that at the market," he added with wry laughter. Just because we're working like beasts in this country doesn't mean we're not human beings. "I'm black and I'm proud," he declared. He rattled on the whole time without taking a look in my direction, like a man who's told his story more than once. The listener hardly matters. Then finally he turned around and saw who I was, and surprise crossed his face.

"I read your book."

His voice was clipped. Beware of taxi drivers who've read your book. Most of the time, they read it at the wheel. A good book to read when you're driving has lots of short chapters and plenty of dialogue. The kind of book I like, too.

"Can I ask you a question?"

"Of course."

"Why did you write that book?"

The question came shooting out of his mouth like a bullet and hit me between the eyes. I wasn't expecting it. Usually, in a bookstore, the book just sits there. You pick it up or you don't. But I kept my cool; I'm used to it. He pretended to pay attention to the road, but I could feel his ears grow unusually long; here was a man ready to listen.

"You'd rather not answer ... I can imagine why."

What could he possibly imagine? Every black in this damned country thinks that each of their fingernail parings is a bomb that will bring down America.

"What's wrong with the book?" I asked a little timidly.

My question caught him off guard. His neck gave an involuntary shake. He wheeled around and the car nearly climbed onto the sidewalk.

"It is the book of a traitor!"

He slammed the steering wheel with the palms of his hands. His right foot jammed the accelerator. It was 2:49 on his dashboard clock.

"Sometimes I think I understand you: I figure you wrote that piece of shit to make money. It's hard, I know, it's plenty hard. No one will give you a break unless you're ready to sell your soul. But for that, you need a buyer."

"In my case," I said, "I'm not looking for a buyer. It's already sold."

"That's right. You're part of the system."

"That's one way of looking at it."

63

He practically jumped into the back seat. He wasn't the kind you could easily contradict.

"What are you talking about?"

"All writers are traitors, in one form or another."

"Stop spewing out those mindless clichés," he ordered.

"It's hard for everyone. The competition is fierce, like in the taxi business. At least you need a licence to drive a cab. Anyone can write."

He seemed almost touched by the comparison. For a minute I thought he was going to smile.

"That was before," he nodded.

"Before what?"

"Now, anyone can buy a licence. Driving a cab isn't the trade it used to be."

I took a look around. His car was very clean, I'll grant him that. He had pinned up photos of Marcus Garvey, Patrice Lumumba, all the great Third World leaders. His taxi was a history lesson on wheels.

"Still," he said, shaking his head, "that's no reason to betray your race."

"When you're not a genius, strip-tease is the only thing that'll bring in the customers."

He spat out the window and put the pedal to the floor, trying to scare me to death. The police are never there when you need them.

"Would you mind repeating that?" he asked mockingly. "I'm no intellectual and I don't catch onto those real refined things."

I don't know a single Third World cab driver who isn't an intellectual. You get into their car, and they immediately start discussing Senghor or Césaire with you.

"Okay, I confess, I write because I want a feeling of power, which is what you're after when you drive like a madman. It's exactly the same process. I want to win the power-relations game, and I'm ready to do anything to get to the top."

There, I hit the mark, using weapons of his choice. He's a man of violence; violence is the only language he understands. His face grew the slightest bit softer, barely visible to the naked eye.

"Why not be the reader's companion instead?"

"The reader's no friend; he's just an illusion. He wants to talk about his life, too. He has a story, and he wants to scream it out to the rest of the world. If I'm going to keep him locked in a room for three or four hours listening to my story, it had better be good."

"Why don't you use your energy to lift up your race?"

"And be in opposition to the very essence of literature?"

"How's that?"

"I don't write on commission."

"You mean you don't want to help defend your people who've been humiliated for centuries?"

"That doesn't make for good writing."

"Africa has a rich history, and black writers have an obligation to communicate it to the rest of the world."

"Exactly my point: I'm a writer of the present. I try to discover bits of the past in the present. Maybe you're right. There must be other blacks who can display the treasures of our race, but I'm not one of them. I'm not the one for the job. All I care about is the fall, decadence, frustration, bitterness, the bile that keeps us alive."

"Admit it: you just want to make money."

"Like everybody else. Literature is a trade by which I support myself. Why doesn't anyone put the question to engineers or doctors or lawyers? I said it already: I write because I want to be famous and enjoy the privileges that famous people enjoy. For instance, getting all those girls who once were out of reach."

The taxi drove through the night. The driver had no answer. A snaking vein in his temple pounded. Manifestly, he was thinking.

"Why not reconcile the two? Make money while trying to pay homage to your race, if you see what I mean."

"Commerce and noble sentiment are irreconcilable."

"Some people do it," he cackled.

"I suppose you mean Wole Soyinka, the Nobel Prize winner."

"Among others."

That's the way blacks are. Whenever one of their kind distinguishes himself somewhere on the globe, they know all about it.

"Listen," I said, "I don't have Soyinka's talent. He's a writer who's going to go down in history. I'd rather be read by people who can't stand me. If you kick a dog, don't expect him to love you, but at least he'll pay attention when you're in the neighborhood. Get the picture?"

He nodded. But a second later, he burst out, "Why do you keep exploiting those clichés about blacks?"

"They're public property. Everybody has the right to work that vein."

"But you're an exploiter—"

"Like everybody else. What do writers do? They devour those closest to them."

"Would you rather have been a white writer?"

"Not at all. It has nothing to do with racism. It's just more convenient to be a black one these days. People are willing to listen to us. We have a new language. People are beginning to tire of the eternal triangle of wife, husband and lover. They're ready to drop everything to hear a new story. We can even take the old saw of adultery and sharpen it up. Make the lover black, and the whole equation goes crazy; America hangs on for dear life."

"If you hate America so much, why don't you go somewhere else?"

"I have the same right as anyone else to be here. I paid my dues. Don't forget: I don't want to destroy America, I just want my piece of the pie—and no crumbs, please. And I'm very level-headed about it."

He laughed for the first time, healthy laughter, a little nervous at first, then veering into something strident at the top. Then it began a joyous descent, heart-felt, alive, laughter that came from the soul.

"It's simple," I said to him, speaking at the same time to the millions of blacks. "Why should I love you? You don't love me. Just because you're black doesn't mean I have to love you. Blacks are the first to call for my destruction."

He turned and gave me an understanding look, as if a light had just gone on in his world.

"I know what it's like, you're going through a rough time … You'll see, it'll come back."

He was the quick-tempered kind of guy who calms down

as soon as anyone else raises his voice.

"What'll come back?" I asked, amazed by his sudden change in tone.

"You know." He looked embarrassed. "Your humanism, your sense of fraternity. We blacks don't know how to hate. We don't have the chromosome of hatred in our bodies."

Those were the limits of his encouragement. The taxi pulled over and stopped at the curb. I paid and got out. Another fare took my place. A white guy. I heard the Nigerian begin his routine.

"I'm an African. To be exact, I was born in Nigeria. In my opinion, all blacks are African. We all came from the first African man and woman, but the Western World ..."

The taxi made a U-turn and headed uptown.

Why Must a Black Writer Write about Sex?

There's always some guy running around like a chicken with its head cut off, and he's always best friends with the bartender. Inevitably, he's a first-class pain in the ass, too.

"Can I get you a drink?"

The next time some guy asks you that question, tell him no. And look the other way.

"No, thank you."

"It's on me."

"No, I really don't want anything more."

"Do it for me."

"All right, just one."

I had no reason to accept. I had enough on me to buy a drink, I didn't like the guy's looks, and I didn't feel like drinking anyway.

"What'll you have?"

"A Cognac."

"One Cognac," he yelled at the top of his lungs to the bartender who was standing right in front of us.

The bartender took the order in his blasé manner and picked up the dusty bottle.

The guy turned and stared at me. These days, I've been noticing that a lot of people do that.

"You don't like champagne? I think I read that somewhere."

"No one ever inquired into the subject."

"Hey, Harry," he called to the bartender, who had the usual bartender name, "forget the Cognac. Bring us a bottle of champagne."

Typical. The behavior of a man who has just made the wholly reasonable decision to kill himself. The classic downward spiral. He separated from his wife. She wants custody of the kids and won't even grant him visiting privileges. This very day, the judge awarded her what she wanted. Now, he's intent on celebrating the court's decision with a bloodbath. An ordinary barroom story.

"Champagne!" he bellowed at the bartender, as if announcing his approaching death.

The bartender, slightly stooped, in his mid-fifties, his suit a bit tight, red bow-tie. His movements were slow but efficient. Everything's A-okay. He didn't understand his customer's death-knell. Perhaps he was inured to the cry of the soul. Then again, maybe nobody cried out, maybe my ears are too sensitive, maybe I'm prone to hearing cries. Maybe that's the usual routine, though I couldn't quite get used to the guy's shouts. Maybe the guy puts on this show every Thursday night, calling for champagne to attract the female of the species.

Which was how it turned out.

70

"Bring three more glasses and a bottle, Harry … Harry, I'm talking to you, three more glasses and one of your special bottles. Harry's a gem," he concluded with a shout.

The guy drummed his finger on the bar to spur Harry into action. Harry and his imperturbable snail speed.

One of the girls called out, "No, Harry, make that three glasses. You know I can't take champagne, Bob."

A shadow crossed Bob's face. Bob is his name; a guy like that has to be called Bob. The shadow was brief but perceptible: someone has refused to kneel down before the great god Champagne. In front of cool, flowing money, money that bubbles over. Champagne is more than a drink; it's a way of celebrating. The big show that impresses the little minds in any bar in any one-horse town on this globe. Have you ever ordered champagne in a bar in Shanghai or Vienna? Instant success. It's like a rock star ripping off his shirt in a small town in Texas. I stole a glance at Bob and printed the image of his face in my brain. Bullet head, horsey face, heavy eyelids crisscrossed by tiny red veins. This man isn't contemplating suicide; he's already there.

"Aren't you having anything?" I asked the girl who had turned down the champagne and, for that reason alone, had become immediately likable.

"I'll have a Perrier and an aspirin, if you're buying."

"Do you have a headache?"

"Worse than that—a killer migraine. Don't worry, I'm used to it. I've had migraines since I was nine."

Crazy, isn't it, but I've always been attracted by girls who

71

suffer from migraines. In general, they're thin, intellectual and very hung up.

The bartender came by with another bottle of champagne. I was wrong about Bob. All that interested him were the two girls, knock-outs if you like the tall, thin blonde type. Thursday night girls. He poured champagne with the casualness of someone fishing in an aquarium. The street door opened and closed. Your average Thursday night in a bar in America.

"What are you doing in a joint like this?" the girl asked me.

"I stopped in for a drink. That's an acceptable reason."

"This isn't your kind of place."

"So you say."

Bob slipped his left hand around her shoulder as he carried on the conversation with two other girls. Mr. Cool. Calmly, she detached his arm from her shoulder.

"You know I can't stand champagne," she reminded Bob, pressing her fingertips to her temple. A typical migraine-sufferer pose. Bob considered her a moment or two, then put a couple feet between them. He knew he had no claim on her. We were free to have our conversation.

"I'd like to ask you a question."

"Yes?"

I expected the worst.

"I read your book ..."

"Yes?"

"I'm afraid to say it because I don't want you to take it the

72

wrong way … Well, here goes: how come sex is the only thing you talk about?"

"Let's be more specific: I talk about the explosive nature of sexual relations between black men and white women."

"Do you think it's always that way?"

"What way?"

"Explosive. Isn't that a bit vain?"

The irony in her smile could lay a city to waste.

"Of course," I answered, trying to match her smile, "there are exceptions."

"You make it seem like it's always about sex."

"And power, too. Isn't that right?"

"Not always. My lover is African, and let me assure you that what goes on between us has nothing to do with sex."

"What's it have to do with?"

"I don't think that's any of your business," she shot back, claws out.

"You have to admit it's an unusual combination: a tall blonde and a big black man."

"What's so exceptional about that?" she raged.

"There's nothing wrong with sex, you know."

"What about feelings? That's why I hated your book so much. I believe there are always feelings in any human relationship. We're not just a collection of organs. As far as I'm concerned, there always have to be feelings."

"I believe you, but that's over my head as a writer. It's not my department. Why don't you tell your story? That might help balance my version of things. I put forward the sexual black hungering for white skin; you can counter with the sentimental black."

73

"You don't take anything seriously. It's not good to be like that." She paused. "He did try ..."

"Who?"

"My lover. No publisher wanted his manuscript."

"Maybe it wasn't good ... I don't know, too sentimental, too complacent."

Her face hardened.

"Go ahead, say it! The only reason your stories sell is because whites find them reassuring. They can read them and go on thinking that blacks are nothing but walking penises."

"Which isn't a false interpretation."

"When are you going to stop provoking people and spit out all your bile once and for all? No human being can keep inside all the suffering I feel in you."

"I love Catholics! Such a sense of suffering! Seriously, I'm not provoking anyone. I'm just analyzing the clichés about sexuality. Interracial sexuality is a good subject, and I happen to be looking for that kind. At first, I wanted to destroy those clichés—how naive of me! It didn't take me long to come to a conclusion that literally terrified me: most of the clichés about sex between black men and white women are true. The whole story is true. At first I was frightened, then I gathered my wits and started to communicate the results of my inquiry to my readers. I'm a writer, a reporter of human relations."

"As long as it suits your purpose."

The bartender finally brought her an aspirin. She went on massaging her temples. Her suffering held so much charm.

"I hated your book so much ... You'll never know how much I hated it."

"But you read it. That's what counts."

Slowly, she closed her eyes.

"I had just met Ibrahim. I'd never felt such a powerful and pure feeling in my life. I worshipped him; I still do. Then, bang, your book shows up. I did everything I could to keep it out of my father's way. Unfortunately, that's all they talked about on the TV, the radio, in the newspapers. I spent hours tearing out the articles about your book, turning off the TV when I knew they were about to talk about it. I was about to have a breakdown."

"Why? Is your family racist?"

"No. But whatever I share with Ibrahim concerns us alone. I didn't want to discuss it with my father, especially with your book in mind. And I didn't want my mother to think I might be one of those white girls you talk about in your book. One of those girls who has only black lovers. I felt sullied by your book."

Her face was tense with a terrible effort.

"Why did you take it so personally?"

"All that business about sex … You seem to be suggesting that white women who go out with black men do so because no white man will have them. Don't you think that's insulting for the woman?"

"And for the man, too. It's insulting, but it's reality. When you've finished dancing and drinking and smoking and spending the evening misplacing your conscience, that's the reality you wake up with the morning after."

"What about love?"

"I told you, it's not up my alley. That feeling is for people of the same race and class and religion. I was about to say the same sex, too. Maybe that's the true secret of love: the marriage of the similar."

"What kind of nonsense is that? That's worse than apartheid!"

"In love, there's no room for justification. You look, and you fall in love. Only sex can transgress."

"I refuse to accept that."

"To each his truth. I can tell you this, though: as a writer, I can't afford the luxury of love. If I write a book about a love affair between a black man and a white woman, no one will buy it! Either that, or they'll read it all wrong."

"How's that?"

"If I describe their visit to the woman's parents' house, who are white, of course, readers will patiently await the confrontation, and if there's no outbreak, they'll figure they've been ripped off. The slightest remark—'Mother, why didn't you set out the white plates?'—and we're off and running. The book would be totally unreadable because it would be read differently, depending on the race, class or religion of the reader."

"I'm sorry, but I can't accept such a cynical vision of things. It's suffocating."

"It's not my fault if things are going so badly. But it's my job to say how they are."

"I think deep down you like it."

"They say you're supposed to like your job."

"Is it possible that, one day, a black writer might write about something else besides sex?"

"It's possible—if he gives up being a black writer."

Why Do Black Writers Prefer Blondes?

The girl sitting next to me at the bar closed the magazine she had been half-heartedly paging through. The bar is patronized by TV actresses, writers on the way up and anorexic models. North American girls are starving themselves to death. If you want to project the slender look, you have to be absolutely skinny.

Coolly, the girl slipped the magazine back into her purse which sat at the foot of her stool. Then slowly she eased off it and moved towards the ladies' room. I watched her walk, head down, as if she wanted to pass unnoticed. Despite the attempt, she lost none of her sensuality. Every movement of her body gave off that kind of energy, as if she were leaping into the world. The less attention she tried to attract, the more she soaked up the men's voracious stares. And the women's, too. The hundred meters between the barstool and the washroom was the theater of her life. My blood rushed towards the organs concerned. Her satin-white back was the final image before the door closed behind her. Fade to black. We all knew she was there, behind the door. Time stood still. How long had she been in there? A half-hour? She returned, completely made up. She didn't need to in order to turn our hearts upside down. What was she trying to do? Put out a fire with a flame-thrower? She took her place on the stool again, crossing her legs high up, nearly to where her thighs branch out. That should be prohibited in public places, the way carrying a loaded firearm is. She lit a cigarette, ready for the battle of the sexes, a war that has killed and maimed more than all others combined. I forgot to mention that she's a true blonde with endlessly long legs and a mocking smile pulling at her lips. *The* blonde, the old unforgotten dream, despite the last fifteen years of feminist saber-rattling. The blonde is the natural enemy of feminism, which has done everything to destroy her in the hearts and minds of men at the end of the millennium. In America, the blonde has had to face the cruelest and most pitiless barrage, for America is her throne. The blonde goddess doesn't exist in Norway or Sweden, where most women are blonde; she is purely an American invention—like the black. Today, we can confirm that she has braved the worst storms (the terrible 1970s and 1980s) without losing a golden hair from her head. Today, the blonde is back, as radiant as the dawn. The future is hers, and she won't share it with anyone. Carefully, I inspect the specimen next to me. I want to see how she works. I want to know how the most fantastic dream machine created by the American male functions.

The battle is raging on several fronts. Her bag, which she keeps rummaging through as if she expected to find an oil well

78

or a gold bar inside. The ordering of a complicated cocktail from the bartender who has seen this kind before. And the short-term plan of returning to the ladies' room. Why, asks the fish that's already hooked, go to the bathroom twice in less than fifteen minutes? An old strategy, brother. It has to do with movement. She breaks off the detailed description of the cocktail and scampers off to the ladies again. As long as she took to cover the hundred meters the first time, now she tries to equal Carl Lewis' Olympic record for the distance. A blinding flash of light, the dazzled faces, a surprise orgasm. My imagination follows her. I don't make a habit of going into the ladies' room, but sometimes my mind can't help but follow. What do they do when the door closes behind them? Are they still goddesses? Is a urinating blonde still sexy? Do they do it like everybody else? Does a fake blonde do it like a real one, and if there is a difference, what is it? Do blondes go to the bathroom to catch their breath, or simply disappear from our sight for a moment? I picture her standing in the middle of the little room, furtively glancing at her imaginary stopwatch. Sun Tzu in his treatise *The Art of War* quotes old Ts'ao Ts'ao: "Attack the void, storm nothingness, outflank his defence, strike him where he least expects it." No one can go to the bathroom that often—except blondes. The blonde is a special class of being. First principle: she knows it. Second principle: if you know it, too, you know everything. I am watching her with such attention because she is one of America's most powerful fantasies, the very heart of our most extravagant dreams. This obscure object of desire is the being closest to light. A light that seems to illuminate her from within. Porcelain skin, the smell of cow's milk. The smell of milk is what attracts the black man. That kind of woman (blonde, long sculpted legs, that lightly mocking smile) constitutes the failure of my life. Not only have I lost the battle, I've been humiliated in my very identity. Don't forget Ts'ao Ts'ao: "One rarely returns from that field." They literally ignored me for two decades. They looked upon me unseeingly, making me feel like a smooth, blank wall, without relief. The eye has no reason to linger there. In other words, you don't exist. How did they develop that capacity for contempt? They're never nervous, no need to hurry. They do not desire; they are desired. Their faces are calm. No false movement nor feeling in their eyes. Nothing like the redhead quivering like a fish on a hook. This is the blonde warrior-woman. In this fight to the finish, you're sure to lose if you don't have a big handbag nearby and the option of rushing off to the ladies' room as often as necessary. What are the weapons at my disposal as I prepare to face her? Just about none. Admit it, I can't even play on the same field, I'm not even in the same league. To put it crudely, a blonde with long legs and a mocking smile (I'm not talking about the dizzy kind) always destroys me. I am allowed to look, but my pleasure ends there, a spectator in her theater of cruelty. She doesn't need to bat an eyelash; already an intricate ballet is swirling around her, a choreography with all male dancers who are remarkably similar. From the wings, you can sense the other girls who've been abandoned, their eyes shining with hatred. America, brother (I'm talking about the Northern half), is divided up between real blondes and fake blondes. Marilyn was fake. So is Madonna. That's how bad it's gotten. Marilyn and Madonna, the two most powerful fantasies of the post-war period, are fake blondes. What about the real kind? I sing you, black impotence! If the blonde is a bombshell all by herself, what about the encounter of the black man and the blonde? The bomb goes off. Meanwhile, the white man rages. He's been wounded in the heart, in the intimacy of his memory. Black man, blonde woman. The blonde represents the whiter-than-white. The Black-Blonde couple is too potent. The inferior with the superior's woman. A rare coupling, rarer than pure diamond. The two extremities of the spectrum. Light and shadow. Absolute complementarity.

She returns. Her eyes glide over me, then stop. She saw me! Her face dissolves with infinite slowness, coming apart by degrees. Then she bestows a smile free of contempt.

"Haven't I seen you somewhere?"

"I really couldn't tell you."

"I know!" she all but screams.

She starts laughing so hard she holds onto her sides. Then she dives into her bag without removing her rear end from the stool. Her ass is an insolent arrow pointed in my direction. She comes back with a magazine, pages through it feverishly then locates the article with my picture. The photo where I'm sitting on a bench in the Carré Saint-Louis with my old Remington on my lap. She displays the magazine without a word. How many words is a photo in a big American magazine worth? She's speechless. The photo of the guy sitting next to her. The journalist came to my house to do the interview. I spent the whole day with her and a laid-back, California-style photographer. He was crazy about me. I was crazy about her. I always fall for powerful women. The journalist wasn't blonde, but she worked for a major magazine, and she did her job well. Mine was to try and get her into bed. The photographer buzzed around us like a tsetse fly. Her tape recorder ran for hours and hours (six TDK cassettes), and he took hundreds of photos. All that for a short piece that didn't even take up a quarter-page. Once the job was done, they disappeared. And now my picture shows up in this large-circulation magazine, and this blonde woman, totally inaccessible a minute ago, can't take her eyes off me. America strikes again, in her own way. Success is all that counts, and American success is the only real kind. I wonder how many blondes I could pick up, at this very moment, with this simple quarter-page article and photo from an American magazine. The question makes my head spin. The prospects are dizzying. Now I understand why big American magazines take their time before publishing an article. Every week, I paged through the magazine to see if my picture was there. Every time, disappointment! Another's face stared out at me. Lord, how many young writers want to make it on this planet? They come streaming in from around the world, dreaming of success, American-style. God, I hate those competitors! Finally, on page thirty-six, at the top right, the article by that woman who came to interview me an eternity ago. I was just complaining to myself about how that bitch America was ripping off the Third World again. America thinks she's the center of the known universe, which is why I hate her so intensely. But it's true: America *is* the center of the known universe, and for once, I'm glad that's true. How much does that poor blonde matter compared to the fact that my photo is being distributed around the world at this very moment? I don't know what "around the world" means to you, but for me, it's the only way to shake off my folkloric image. Concretely, it means that if I get on a plane for Vienna, let's say, some European city I've never been to, there's a very good chance I'll run into some blonde (there are even blondes in Africa, brother) who will recognize me right off the bat and be ready to give herself to me. That's America, brother, and for just this once, she's on my side. How long will it last? That's another story.

"Is that really you?" the girl asks, her voice quavering ever so slightly.

"Yes."

As laconic as I wanna be.

"Why *do* black writers prefer blondes?"

That was the title of the article. Racial and sexual issues, as always. Their explosive combination. America can't get enough of it, and I'm ready to meet the demand.

"I really don't know why," I answer with false modesty. "Opposites attract, I suppose."

"That's not what you said in the article," she tells me with a broad smile, the kind of smile that blondes reserve for winners.

"Since you know my answer ..."

She gives me another smile.

"What makes you think blondes are attracted by blacks?"

A question devoid of irony.

"The purity of the colors."

She shoots me a glacial look. The young American blonde deploys her final weapons. I don't budge. I've spent my life observing haughty blondes. I know how to go about it. Don't move a muscle. I've got the big end of the stick, and I'm not letting go. It's up to her to keep the conversation going. Her eyes are full of night and terror, and that doesn't happen to her very often. She has to learn fast. It's good when the order of things is shaken up. All it takes is a short article (with a photo, all the same) in a large-circulation American magazine, and everything changes. To think that I used to despise those mind-numbing periodicals and their brainless machinery! To think that once I looked down on those trend-following girls who always have their noses in a glossy magazine that smells like a French whorehouse on a Saturday night! With those pictures of colorless, odorless, tasteless, antisepticized models. Suddenly, the print runs of those magazines fascinate me. Only four million copies? I was sure they printed at least twelve mil-lion! Let's do a little arithmetic. Of those four million readers (go ahead, multiply the figure by three), there must be at least one million blondes. And of those one million blondes (of course, three-quarters of them are fake), a little more than two hundred thousand now know that I exist. Yet worry has wormed its way into my euphoria: is there a Chinese version of the same magazine? I wouldn't look down my nose on two or three million Chinese girls. Meanwhile, I've totally forgotten the journalist who interviewed me; she was but a stepping-stone to glory. A little brown-haired girl with no distinguishing charac-teristics. As you climb the rungs of the Judeo-Christian ladder, those at the bottom progressively lose their stature. Maybe they really *are* that small. Only yesterday, that girl seemed beautiful and untouchable; now, she's as dull and useless as an unplugged refrigerator. How could we have ever fallen for her? When will we be able to say, *She's the one I want, the one I've always wanted, the one I really want?* We fear that declaration like the plague, for death cannot be far behind. The death of all desire. Luckily, there's a long way to go. The living keep on marching. There's only two sides, brother: the quick and the fallen.

I stare out across the room. The waitress stumbles as she goes by, but she doesn't lose her smile. How can these people keep smiling as the wheel of fortune rolls over them? Their motto: smile through the pain. The waitress's pretend smile is the modest triumph of a false art of living. Don't listen to me, I'll say anything that comes into my head. There's always something jumping out of the grab-bag. Sometimes I talk to one person while thinking of another. Right now, I'm looking at a fragile spider slipping down Prince's showy, perverted poster for *Diamonds and Pearls*, while I listen to two girls behind me debating about Madonna. I can't sit still. My spirit goes wandering. The goal is to avoid the only subject that really counts: I haven't written a single line since I've gotten famous. I don't even want to think about it, and I've managed to keep anyone from suspecting the truth.

"What's it like to be famous?"

"It's really nothing at all."

"Really?"

"Really."

That's the definition of impotence: losing the right to complain. Everybody thinks I'm rich, famous and happy.

"I feel so strange …"

"Yes?" I turn to my blonde bar-mate. "Why is that?"

Nervous laughter. She rummages through her bag.

"I don't know ... Maybe because I'm sitting next to you. You must think that's stupid."

I shake my head and give her a hypocritical smile.

"I'm sure it's not the first time it's happened to you."

"What's happened to me?"

"That a girl talks to you this way."

"What way?"

"Really, you don't understand a thing!"

On the contrary. I want her to get a taste of her own medicine. When you're too used to playing the hunter, you forget how the prey thinks. The hunter forgets that he, too, is being observed, followed, analyzed. He thinks only of his hunger. The prey defends its life. Of course, the two have something in common.

"You're so silent."

More silence.

"Maybe I'm boring you," she ventures sadly.

The silence lengthens.

I look at her face, serious and tense. She awaits an answer, some kind of sign from me. I could have crushed her, pitilessly, the way she did unto others a dozen times tonight. But her openness, her sudden naiveté, her freshness touched me. This isn't a fantasy sitting next to me, but a poor girl who happens to be tall and beautiful, everything for which there's no forgiveness in America. A poor girl who's come to the city to try to earn her living with what the Good Lord gave her. Men picked her out of the crowd and told her why. In no time at all, she became a war criminal in a battle where no prisoners are taken. Now, it's her turn to suffer the slings and arrows. That's how the wheel turns.

She's squeezing a tiny piece of bread between her fingers. Her eyes are lost. Her voice is distant, a little hoarse with tension. The voice of a different woman.

"This morning, my horoscope told me I was going to meet someone important. The day went by; nothing happened. Tonight I didn't really want to go out because I have a photo session tomorrow. But I felt like I had to. I threw on some clothes and came here, as if someone was urging me along: *you have to go there.* I get here, I have a drink or two, I buy this magazine next door, which I almost never do. Usually I read at night, in bed, before I go to sleep. I come back to the bar, I order a drink, I open the magazine, and guess what story I come to first? I thought the title was really funny. I started reading the interview. I like the way you say things. You're a little crude, but I can feel the tenderness behind it, am I right? I put the magazine back in my bag and start thinking about you. It's funny, I thought about you because you make me think of myself. You reveal so much of yourself that when I read the interview I wanted to do the same. It's easier that way, when you don't hide anything. You feel you can face anything the world has to give."

A silence pregnant with promise.

"I was wondering what I was doing here with all those guys who just want to get into my pants."

Count me in!

87

"A lot of memories, things I've kept hidden, came to the surface. That's not like me, and you can believe it. I hardly ever look back. It hurts too much. I don't know why, but I couldn't stop thinking of those things, really private things. And then," she laughed freely, "I told myself that I wanted to talk with you. A real conversation, not just a strategy where one side thinks of ways to screw the other. You know what I mean?"

Too bad. I was beginning to build up some serious intentions towards that little treasure under her black mini-dress.

"The woman who wrote the article said you never stopped laughing during the interview. I don't think she really understood. Maybe I'm going out on a limb, but something tells me that you're sad underneath, terribly sad, even sadder than me, and that's saying a lot, because I can count the number of times I've been happy on one hand since I was born. Funny, but reading your words cheers me up. You can't imagine ... Maybe I'm embarrassing you, so excuse me ... It's like I'm freeing myself from a weight. I don't want to bore you with my problems, but you're the only person I can talk to about that. Usually, men run like hell as soon as you talk about something personal. In my profession, you know, you don't often get a chance to talk honestly with someone, especially with a man." She laughed bitterly. "As soon as you show who you really are, they lose interest. Am I talking too much? Tell me if I am. My mother says that's what drives men away, especially the ones you'd like to keep." She smiles sadly. "As for the others, they wouldn't go away if I paid them! I guess I'm unlucky! They say you have to cultivate a mysterious side if you want to hold onto a man, but that's not easy if you're like me. I should stop talking and give you a chance to answer. Funny, a half-hour ago, I said to myself that I'd give anything to listen to you, and now that you're here, all I do is talk. Don't judge me ... Funny, but I can't stop myself. It's like an itch, I have to scratch it. All people think about is fucking, but for me, talking is much more intimate. Most guys you go to bed with, and here I'm counting myself," she smiled sweetly, "you really don't want to talk with them. But when I meet someone, someone interesting like you, someone I really want to talk to, I shouldn't say this, but I really don't want to go to bed with them afterwards, I feel all emptied out ... It's stronger than making love, I can tell you that. You see, when I talk with you, it's like we made love, right here in front of everybody." She blushed to the tip of her ears. "I shouldn't be telling you all this, I'm trusting you, you know, and now I'm really going too far ... I'm not usually this way, at work they call me the Mute. Stop me if you have the slightest respect for me ..."

Which is what I did. I went to the washroom to catch my breath and think about this infernal situation. I had lost control over my life. My real life. I sat down on the toilet and a terrible depression fell upon me. My body was a spiral of pain. My bones, my belly, my back. As if I'd been put through a meat grinder. Suddenly I felt absolutely alone in the American night, and that's the worst thing that can happen to anyone. Solitude is the natural culmination of an American life.

Why Do You Write?

The friend who turned me onto this journalism job came into my workroom where I'd been holed up for an hour or two. The heat was unbearable. I was working bare-chested and sweating bullets.

"There's beer in the fridge," I told him.

"What are you doing?"

"Typing."

"So I see. You're doing your America piece?"

"I'm getting my notes together."

He swallowed half the beer in one gulp, pulled up a chair and sat reading my notes for a minute or two.

"Don't you think your blonde business is a little out of date?"

"What do you mean?"

"Oh, you know ..."

"Fashion doesn't interest me. I like to write about things that seem out of date. If we don't talk about something, we think it's stopped existing, but American society hasn't budged from the 1950s. It's still running on the same myths, and the blonde is one of America's founding myths."

"Things have happened since then, you know."

"Like what?"

"I don't know ... Kennedy, feminism, Martin Luther King, the sexual revolution."

"All of that concerns about one half of one percent of the population. Its effect is almost nil."

"Everyone I know is divorced."

"Everyone you know? You mean three hundred people, brother? Here we're talking about three hundred million."

"So what?"

"America's a big place."

"What are you going to do now, oh, wise one?"

"I'm going to hit America's road. I'm going to keep on writing down what I see, not what people tell me to see. I'm a freelancer, man. A street reporter."

PART THREE

How?

How Can a Black Writer Find His Way in This Jungle?

I was sitting in the park thinking about it all. For instance, what can I talk about next?

"Me."

"What?"

"Talk about me."

I turned around. A young black woman was standing there. Insolent mouth, red fingernails, firm breasts. A burning package of rock-hard desire, held in check by an iron will. The kind that won't let go of the piece she's sunk her teeth into. Pearly white teeth, by the way, but that's a cliché.

"Excuse me, but I'm not following."

"How could you not? You're a writer, and you're looking for a subject. Well, I'm the subject."

"Why should I write about you?"

"You give too much press to white women, if you ask me."

"You have no reason to envy the coverage, I assure you."

"Curse me or praise me, as long as you talk about me and spell my name right—that's what they say."

"What's your name?"

"Erzulia."

"You know that's the name of a dreadful voodoo goddess."

"Of course. And I can be just as cruel as she is."

"I suppose you're used to getting what you want."

She smiled briefly. Scarcely moved the corner of her mouth.

"Let's say I agree to write about you ... But you understand, this isn't Oxfam or CARE here. There are no holds barred. Would you agree to any kind of portrait?"

"I don't know how to write, but I know what a book is. I can't stand complacency. When a book isn't honest, I throw it away."

"I can tell you understand the problem."

"I'm no fool. I know, I look young ..."

"Why do you want to be in a book when you know very well you might get massacred?"

"I want to be famous. That's it. I'm no different from anybody else."

"Everybody isn't famous."

"Those who aren't don't exist."

A pause.

"I see ..."

"Especially in my line of work. I have three strikes against me: I'm black, I'm a woman, and I'm not famous."

"But you're sexy."

"They know they can have that for free—if not from me, then from someone else. Guys don't give you anything for that any more. A piece of ass isn't worth a red cent. Besides, they're all fags. Nothing shaking in that neighborhood."

96

"Why me?"

"I'm tired of listening to black writers advertising for white women. White writers only talk about white women. So now with black writers onto white women, too, we don't stand a chance."

"We're only trying to protect you."

"Go fuck yourself."

"Maybe you're not a proper subject."

"How can that be?"

"If a white writer starts fantasizing about you on the page, he'll be accused of colonialism."

"That *is* a problem ..."

"And if a black writer writes about you, you both end up in the ghetto."

"And when white writers write about white women, which they do one hundred percent of the time, what does that produce? Incest?"

"Now, listen—"

"Don't talk to me like that, you remind me of my father. And that's no compliment, believe you me."

"You don't leave the others much room."

"I'm being honest with you, and I don't give a shit if you like it or not."

"I'm trying to tell you that it's difficult to talk freely about someone who's in an inferior position."

"God, are you complicated! Do you always talk that way?"

"I'm just trying to make myself understood."

"That's right, take me for an idiot."

"I'm saying that a black writer can get away with express-ing his most violent fantasies about white women without creating too large a scandal because the white woman is higher than the black man on the Judeo-Christian social scale. As soon as you get the power to realize your fantasies, it becomes harder to express them."

"You really believe that nonsense? You don't think that machos express themselves? They're all we hear about in the papers, on TV, at the movies. I got it all figured out: all men think about is fucking women, whether they're black, red, white or yellow, rich or poor, big or little, healthy or handicapped, Catholic or Protestant. I know from personal experience."

Her eyes challenged the entire world.

"All men don't think just about women," I said.

She burst out laughing. True, physical laughter, the laughter of someone who's essentially honest.

"You're right. One point for you. All men don't think just about women."

"There's more to life than sex."

"There's only sex," she replied definitively.

The two camps had said everything they had to say on the subject.

"I want you to put me in your book."

"Back to square one! I still believe that a black writer portraying a black female character doesn't provide enough contrast. Why don't you consult a white writer?"

"I'm starting with you."

"Why not a woman? There are women writers around, these days."

"They don't interest me."

"A woman would understand you better."

"Women aren't any good unless they're talking about men."

"That's not my opinion."

"It's not the way you think it is, either. Women have a bone to pick with men. Talking about men gets them mad, and that's when they start getting good."

"I think that women know men better than they know themselves," I argued, "since they spend three-quarters of their time with men."

"You're beating around the bush. Is it too much to ask to be in your book?"

"I don't know if you've ever heard of freedom of expression."

"You know what you can do with your freedom of expression! You wrote a book to get famous; I want the same thing you do. I want to be in your next book for the same reason. I don't care what you write about me, and to be perfectly honest, I don't even think I'll read your book. If you weren't famous, I wouldn't waste my time telling you my life story. That's all I'm asking ... Check you later!"

She headed towards a group of musicians playing by the park entrance. I watched her. She was facing the sun. Then she turned and came striding back towards me.

"What do you care whether I'm in your book or not? I've got everything I need to be in a book, and you can't imagine what I might do!"

How Can an Honest Black Writer Work in These Conditions?

I'm supposed to meet my publisher today. He's waiting for me at his office. From there we'll go to a restaurant close by. A discreet little restaurant, not too expensive, where we can talk in peace. He'll drink wine; I'll order beer. We'll take our time eating and speak of many things. I love *foie gras*; he goes for veal.

At the cheese course, he asked anxiously, "Are you working on something?"

"Sort of."

"I see ..."

"A kind of a thing."

"A novel?"

The magic word.

"You could say that. I wouldn't call it a novel."

"But it's not poetry?"

"Nor theater. Don't worry."

"I'm not worrying. Write what you want to."

"As long as it's a novel."

"As long as you write."

"As long as you write."

Things started to heat up, since he was just about sure I wasn't writing anything.

"Are you really writing?"

"I'm making a few notes."

"I see," he said wearily.

The waiter asked if we were ready for desert. I ordered vanilla ice cream and he wanted custard.

We ate in temporary silence.

"I remember," he mused, "a young man who was impassioned by literature. Back then you could talk for hours about Malraux, Baldwin, Borges ... Do you still read them?"

"A little."

"You should do a book about your favorite writers. Something simple, saying why you feel the way you do."

"There are so many books I should write."

"Why take it that way? I'm not pushing you, it's just an idea."

"I know. I was talking to myself."

I concentrated on my dessert. I didn't want to rub salt in his wounds.

"You used to be more timid."

"When was that?"

"When you brought me your first manuscript."

"I was playing it close to the chest."

"There was a strange light in your eyes."

"You're mixing me up with one of your young lady novelists."

"Don't be so cynical."

"That's what success does, old friend."

"Funny, but I don't feel you've really changed. I'm sure

"I hear the publisher speaking."

"Who else should it be?"

"The friend."

"And what would the friend say that would be different from the publisher?"

"That I don't have to write another book, that it's always better to follow your own rhythm, without pushing it or stressing out, that there's more to life than writing books."

"That would be cowardly of me."

"But that's what I'd like to hear right now."

"If I told you that, you'd think I'd stopped believing in your talent."

"What is talent anyway? Everyone talks about it, but no one knows what it is."

"It's what got you out of the factory."

"Sometimes I think I would have been better off staying there."

"You didn't used to say that."

"Excuse me, sir."

The waiter brought the bill and slipped it under a saucer by the publisher's elbow. Here we are, two adults at a restaurant, so why did the waiter give my publisher the bill? I've noticed that every time I eat with a white person, inevitably he gets the bill. A black man is no different from a woman in the waiter's eyes. Which is no doubt the supreme insult for a woman. But when a white woman and a black man are at a restaurant, who gets the honor of the bill? The woman, of course. The black man must be the pimp. The equation is simple: the white man pays for the white woman; the white woman pays for the black man; the black man never takes the black woman out. When are black women around the world going to unite to change this? Maybe it's already begun. In America, the black woman is afraid to hurt her man; after all, he's just getting to his feet after years of oppression, and that's slowing things down. If there's going to be progress in America, everyone knows that black women are going to be in the forefront. They're building the community. Maybe I am ready after all to write a book about the situation of black women in America. The black woman according to a black writer. I'll try that out on my publisher.

"I've started a little something about black women ... The subject's a delicate one."

"What do you mean?"

Smoke began pouring out of his ears.

"It's bad enough talking about white women, so imagine black women. The black woman is the queen of victims. You can't get any more victimized than that."

"And what kind of tone are you going to use?" he asked anxiously.

"It's going to be tough."

"Very tough?"

"Very. No quarter given. The kind of thing that'll make everyone hate me."

"Remember, you still need a handful of readers."

We laughed together like old partners in crime.

"Have you begun?"

"I've got thirty pages or so. A black woman absolutely wants me to write about her."

"Sure. Everybody wants a writer to tell their story."

"But she couldn't care less. She doesn't even want to read

the book."

"That's what she says now, but when the book comes out, she'll be the first to lynch you."

"So you don't think it's a good subject?"

"I don't think anything," he said, acting the part of the prudent publisher. "I'm just playing devil's advocate. You figure it out for yourself. Let me read what you've got."

"It's not ready. I want to be sure it's worth your time."

Why do I get the feeling that my publisher's interest has suddenly dropped off? A few minutes went by before he realized I hadn't written a single word of this imaginary book. He picked up the tab. He had come in search of information and discovered nothing had changed. My stomach was tied in knots; too much *foie gras*, maybe.

Before we stepped into the street, my publisher imparted this last piece of advice.

"Maybe I shouldn't tell you this, but even your enemies think it's time you wrote another book."

The Ten Warning Signs of Fame

I stopped by the Librairie du Square, the corner bookstore, to buy a few magazines, and for the last half hour I've been sunning myself. Doing nothing, thinking of nothing. I page through a woman's magazine: my picture is still there, and it will stay there for the next month. The pleasure of the monthly publication. I'm famous today, which no doubt bugs the hell out of the rest of the planet. Especially those people who didn't even have the time of day for me (except for that Frenchman from Auvergne) back when I was starving to death in that lousy one-room apartment up on the third floor of 3670, Saint-Denis. Right across the street from the Café Cherrier, where I happen to be right now, waiting for the beautiful young actress who has shot to stardom for her work in the Musset play at the Théâtre du Nouveau Monde. That crummy little room, right across the street, is where I wrote my first novel. People have been talking about that book ever since. I could go ahead and write the novel of the century, and people would still talk about the first book. When Jerzy Kosinski died, *Time* described him as the author of *The Painted Bird*—his first book, which he published thirty years before. He might as well have stopped writing. Which wasn't the case. For the public at large, he remained the author of a first novel composed in fever and innocence. Maybe that's what killed him. Every time he came out with a new book, people reminded him of his first one. Garcia Márquez said that he wrote his subsequent books to kill *One Hundred Years of Solitude*. Observe the different methods: Kosinski committed suicide by wrapping a plastic bag around his head, while Márquez preferred to execute his novel. Don't expect a South American to kill himself over a book. Now, you might think I'm going through a minor nervous breakdown. Not at all. Why am I saying not at all? What does not at all really mean? Maybe it means I'm happy, that life is smiling on me, it's all a bowl of cherries, everything's A-okay, and I got what I wanted: to be famous and have all the girls I want. Am I really happy? I should observe myself. Isn't that what writing is? Self-observation? Some people write to be happy. Some books make us happy. But there are no happy writers. If a writer tells you he's happy, he's lying. Like me. We write because there's something missing, a lack in our being. Back when I was writing my first novel, life was simpler: I was missing everything. I lacked wine, food, the laughter of carefree girls, money to pay the rent, free, endless conversations in bars without wondering who would cover the bill. That's why there's so much wine (bad wine at that), so many carefree young girls and laughter in that cursed first novel. Look at Haitian painting and you'll understand. The landscapes all look like the Garden of Eden. The fruit is too perfect. The fish are too big. The children's smiles are too wide. A dream country concocted to replace the real one. Scarcely ten years ago, I

106

started to write my first novel right across the street, in that overheated slum room I shared, back then, with that old monkey Bouba. The 1980s had yet to change the world. Reagan had just taken over. It was the middle of summer in the heart of poverty. I didn't know anyone, and no one knew me. I had just arrived in North America. I didn't know what to do with my life; maybe there was nothing to do with it, or with the fire that burned me. With the mad desire to speak. Gentle reader, beware of a starving young man with a typewriter under his arm. I raged and wrote, morning, noon and evening. The super (a real bastard) wouldn't let me work at night. I set up a little table by the window, looking out on the world I wanted to conquer. Sentences shot out like missiles. I took up position in this redoubt, the better to train my sights upon the enemy. People who glided by in luxury cars, young executives in search of the perfect restaurant, dazzling blondes for whom I didn't exist: the society that had slammed its door in my face. I wasn't writing to change the world; I wanted to change my world. No one can know the rage contained in an empty belly. The man gazing out upon the world from behind the window, plotting terrible vengeance against society. The world in its present state did not please him. On the other side was Reagan who wanted everything for the rich, the insatiable rich. He intended to grab the last piece of bread from the poor man's mouth and give it to the rich. I was preparing to do battle with Reagan—one of the most disastrous of my life. Now, Reagan has disappeared or he's dead, I don't know which, but the rich are richer than ever. My situation has changed, too, I must admit. Back then, when I finished a chapter, I would go out patrolling the rue Saint-Denis. Montreal's cruelest street. I watched people stuffing

107

in tons of food behind restaurant windows. Carefree young men have a detestable habit of stubbing out cigarettes in their full plates of food. Salt in my wounds. I watched them and said to myself that one day, just like Alice, I'd go through the other side and sit down with the rich. How does it feel, man? I'll tell you later. Don't worry about it, because now I'm waiting for a splendid actress (young and blonde, it goes without saying) to share my *salade niçoise*. Words in the wind, brother. I'm talking about a stage actress. The theater, not some down-market celluloid actress with silicone breasts. At the theater, when you admire an actress (physically as well as artistically), you can go see her in her dressing-room after the performance. It's like winning the instant lottery. Whereas in the pictures, you discover, months later, that Julia Roberts' miraculous body that drove you half crazy in *Pretty Woman* was not hers at all. The only problem is that theater actresses are harder to get than film actresses. It's part of their tradition. How often did I dream those dreams as I wandered through the luminous, slummy rooms of this city? I ended up forgetting (we always forget what has most deeply marked us) that I wrote that first novel for this very purpose: to take my place with a beautiful young actress at an outdoor café at two o'clock on a summer afternoon, and chat with her about ... let's see ... why not Claudel? Sumptuous, sensual mysticism. How exquisite Virgil is! And Musset's first fires. But the poet of the summer, the eternal summer of the life of young theater actresses, of love's carmine desire, is Garcia Lorca. Frederico must be read in summer. The waiter approaches, asks me what I need. Nothing, right now. I'm waiting for a friend. She's not late; I'm early. I always show up early. I don't like to be seen arriving. I wait at my ease, like the apostles, who knew what was what, awaited the resurrection of Christ. I watch this world go by. A guy shows up in the park with a young tiger, and everyone crowds around him. A police car slows down. The waiter comes by a second time, but he's obviously not worried about the fact that I haven't eaten or drunk anything since this morning. What interests him is the tip. I understand his motivation and resentment. I understand, but I can't do anything for him. Charity isn't up my alley. I understand the arrogance of café waiters, especially those who work in places that cater to the pseudo-intellectual. Since they've seen so many writers, TV stars and big-time journalists, these guys start thinking that they're big-time waiters themselves, and they'll spit on you if your name isn't shining brightly enough in the papier-mâché heavens of star cafés. The definition of glory: your photo between Marilyn's and Madonna's on the wall. In more practical terms, it means a good table outdoors while a couple of dozen commoners wait in line outside. Naturally, you don't reach this level overnight, or on the strength of a single success. If you forget to pay (that does happen!), no one will charge out after you. The waiter gives me a quick glance. Then she appears, dazzling in her summer dress. Whose idea is it to make dresses that short? She dances towards me in the early afternoon light. I await her with the patience of an egg-timer, though this is hardly the moment to let my eagerness show. Relax, man, in forty seconds she'll be at your table. Forty seconds? An eternity.

How to Relive the Good Old
Days without Nostalgia

She has escaped me. Gone to a meeting with her new director, a schizophrenic. I cross the street to visit my old apartment at 3670, rue Saint-Denis. The buzzer is still missing. I knock on the street door. A young man appears, the new super. The old one, the Greek, has gone back to his native village, or so I'm told. He really wasn't a bad guy. You could do any kind of business you wanted to (drug deals, prostitution, etc.) at any hour of the night, but after ten o'clock in the evening, I wasn't allowed to type a single line. He didn't understand that writing could have some use in life. In a normal building, I can understand, but not in this rat-hole where there wasn't a single family, only whores, belly dancers, topless waitresses and pimps. The nightlife of any great city, people who didn't hit the hay till noon.

"I don't want no noise."

"What difference does it make?"

"People want to sleep."

Where did he think he was, the Ritz Carlton, maybe?

"I'm working, Mr. Zorba."

He hated being called that.

"I told you, I don't want no noise."

"I'm working!"

"Since you're always working, you can pay me the two months you owe!"

That bastard always did have to have the last word! He treated me like a dog because I didn't sell drugs or have girls working the streets for me, because the police never knocked down my door. In his conceptual universe, a man who didn't have a police record must be an informer. What really bugs me is that the fool doesn't even know I got famous from the very book he tried to stop me writing. I'm famous, and he doesn't even know it. It's always that way. We write for vengeance, and meanwhile, the person has died or is long gone. Of course, I speak differently when it comes to the press. I tell them I write to express essential truths lurking in some obscure corner of my soul. But really, the major reason I wrote that little book was to tell that Greek super to screw off, and with him all those pushers who looked at me as if I was worth less than a black-fly. I keep up with them in the yellow press. So-and-So was found floating in the river. His best friend was found in a trash compactor. As for that asshole superintendent, I hope he's dying of malaria somewhere in a swampy village. He truly hated me. He never wanted to replace the cruddy mattress I slept on. Come to think of it, his stupidity and ignorance, the fact that this mediocre, ugly dullard of a man could despise me kept me struggling on through the darkness, even when there wasn't as much as a flicker at the end of the tunnel. His gaze was a constant, terrible, implacable assault on my reason for

111

living. He wounded me to my very heart. Am I a human being or not? That way he had of brushing past me, practically pushing me with his shoulder, without even looking in my direction: that's what I was up against. He was a worthy enemy. He was so at ease in his mediocre, closed world that it terrified me. *What if he was right?* I wondered. Maybe I don't have any talent. But talent didn't concern him; he was interested in something more genetic. He cast my humanity in doubt. I was a mangy dog in his book, and that was the long and short of it. He didn't suspect; he knew. He wondered when I'd start barking. Now if that won't turn you into a writer! I started writing to prove that I wasn't a dog, and that's not just a metaphor. Today I'm a well-known writer, and he's planting tomatoes somewhere in Greece. He doesn't know I'm famous. If he ever thinks of me, he'll conjure up the picture of a dog.

How Did It All Begin?

It all began one day, at noon. I was lying on a stained mattress watching TV when the girl came in. I'd left the door open. I watched her slip into the room. She'd been here two or three times with another girl, a tall thin one who was forever puffing away at a Camel. She went immediately to the fridge to get a beer. There was no beer. There were no onions, no carrots, no milk, no coffee, no lettuce, not even a bottle of water—nothing at all. The refrigerator wasn't unplugged; just empty. The mechanism rattled away for no apparent reason. The girl's look of disgust woke me from a long sleep. The endless sleep of depression. I hadn't moved for the last few days. How can you describe it, how can you describe inaction in a book? It's not easy, brother. You can make it charming in a book, but in reality, it's unliveable. The terrible lie of literature that always made me sick to my stomach. How can you describe the breadless days when nothing happens? If you talk of boredom without boring the reader, are you not betraying the real feeling? I was lying there on a crummy mattress, staring out the window at the sky. I let things take their course, and they were all rushing towards the great black hole of insanity. I woke up because of that look of disgust tainted with pity on the face of a girl who didn't exist for me. Even she felt that way—her disgust was one humiliation too many. It was time to get on my feet again, but that's not easy after a long period of inertia. I appealed to the nostalgia of the vertical position and, that afternoon, stood on my two feet. That evening, I went out for a drink at the Park Avenue bar. The same faces. The same guys were cruising the same chicks, drinking the same drinks and telling the same stupid stories. The kind of thing that makes you wish you'd never gotten out of bed. Sometimes I think it's a fundamental error to ever get out of any bed. Adam, Cham, Jenny, Charlie, the usual suspects. You can travel around the world, and when you return, the same guys will be waiting to pour the same kind of nonsense into your ear. How Charlie stole Cham's chick again and how Adam is writing the novel that will tell all our stories. In other words, I was more depressed than ever, in a kind of convalescence, unprepared for the nocturnal foolishness. I went and sat at a table in the back, practically in darkness. I had been nursing my beer for the last hour when this chick showed up. She pulled up a chair and invited herself to sit down. Okay, so she was drunk, drunker than drunk, to tell the truth. Her tongue was furry, her words completely inaudible. Finally, I understood that she wanted a beer and that she wanted to ask me a question. I was afraid she was offering me her body, because I never say no to that kind of offer, it's a question of principle with me. What she really wanted was to ask me a question, but first she had to have a beer, otherwise … Otherwise, what? I didn't understand the nature of the threat. So what about the question? No, beer first! I motioned to the waitress. Now, let's have the question! She wanted to know what black men said about her behind her back. All that crap just for that? I answered her rudely, and she went staggering away. Those were the kind of evenings America had in store for me back then. But when I got home, in a calmer frame of mind, I asked myself the same question. What do black men say about white women when they're not around to hear? I'd been wanting to write a book for some time, a book that would ask the questions I was ready to confront. One day, a man decides to confront his life. The bull's horns. A lot of people think that all you need to write a book is a piece of paper and a pencil. I say you need a good question, and that one seemed pretty interesting to me at the time. Not too complex, but tough enough. With two strong-willed characters: a black man and a white woman. And a question the white woman asks when she's off-stage. What does the black man say about me when I'm not there? People want to know what others think of them—that's a legitimate desire. Behind the question lies a secret; something must be revealed. From the bottom of my heart, I want to thank that drunk woman for giving me the gift of a question that changed my life. I'll thank her, but I'm not about to share my royalties. People always want to sue you. If I made an admission like that in the United States, I could just imagine the number of alcoholic young women who would show up at my door the next day, accompanied by their lawyers, demanding at least ten percent of my earnings. True, a good question is worth a book, but let's not exaggerate, girls. I think I'd better change the subject ... My lawyer and accountant are waving their arms wildly, they insist I stop this legally sticky conversation. Never combine

115

literature and money. Look at Proust's work; where does money enter into it? Without money, do you think he would have been able to complete his interminable, asthmatic search for time past? Time is money. Time past is money past. Except for Proust's time, which helped the Gallimards in Paris get rich. I bless money and seek out its company. I'm not talking about the company of the wealthy who wasted so much precious time for Truman Capote. (Everybody can't be Proust, dear Truman.) I'm talking about money in its pure state, money itself, paper money and, of course, the ting and whirl of coins. When it gets too hot in summer, the best shelter isn't a church, no matter what they say: it's a bank. The air conditioning is more discreet, and you don't have to listen to the endless complaint of desperate believers telling the rosary of their misfortune. Nothing is worse for a poor man than the presence of other poor people. You feel you're not alone with God, and then there's the nagging issue of whether God's generosity has a limit. Won't all our requests ruin Him? Why don't you go to a bank instead, get in line and leave just before you get to the counter. Of course, you won't be able to keep doing that at the same bank. But don't worry, these days there are more banks than churches. And hallelujah for that!

How to Enjoy Instant Success

"It's me!"

I turned around.

"Oh, no, not you again."

But it was her. Erzulia. The black goddess with the red eyes, the one who'll do anything to get into my book.

"You're looking for someone to help you face success, aren't you?"

"How do you know?"

"I know everything about you. I'm always there. We can share your success, you know."

Her openness always makes me smile.

"You're mistaken. It's not something you can share."

"Why not?" she challenged me.

"Success decides when it will land on you; it doesn't depend on you. You can't just take a little and leave the rest on the table."

"I wouldn't mind a crumb."

"There aren't any crumbs. Either you eat the whole cake, or there's no cake at all."

"What are the choices?"

"It's fight or flight."

"What about you?"

"I'm not sure yet."

"I can help you, you know."

A sly smile. We went walking down the street, towards downtown.

"I can be successful whenever I want to," she announced, stepping up the pace.

The sky was gray but there were plenty of people on the street. I was too lost in my thoughts to pay much attention to Erzulia. What can be done when you're facing a monster that will devour you as surely as failure will?

"I could be successful now if I wanted to," she continued energetically.

If I stopped writing … No, it's an illusion to think you can escape success. The more you try to avoid it, the quicker it'll find you. It can pester you even in the grave. Look at Picasso; you can't even leave one of his pictures as an inheritance. Look at Picasso's kids. Success blindly strikes people, animals, even plants. The lion is successful, while we despise the earthworm. The rose wishes it could escape that burdensome glory that makes people want to cut her thorns off. That's a good one! The same ones who say they love you want to cut off your thorns! Who's that? Everyone who isn't successful and wants to be, and that adds up to quite a number, believe me. I'm not talking about my own case; a writer can never have real success. You have to buy the book, then read it, and that's too complicated for today's citizens. You can listen to a rock musician for free on the radio or watch a TV actor without

118

spending hard-earned cash. I've never had street-level success, the real kind: you show up somewhere and immediately all eyes turn to you. You sit down to eat in a restaurant and a minute later you notice that people are holding their forks the way you hold yours. A horrible synchronization, as if there were only one person in the place. You've been magnified a hundred times. Success, brother, is when the individual's self becomes so strong it forces other selves to capitulate. It's when a guy would trade his life for yours, no questions asked. That's not natural. What *is* natural is that after a while that same guy will start dreaming of murder. Killing the pet of the gods: *you.* Hey, why are people staring at me like that? I'm only a writer.

"See, I told you."

"What are you talking about?"

I looked in her direction and discovered she had taken off her blouse. Her breasts were pointed straight ahead, two death-dealing revolvers shooting streams of bullets into the crowd, man-high.

"Are you crazy?"

"That's what I'd call instant success."

She began laughing. Endless laughter pouring out of her mouth like a many-colored Möbius strip.

"See," I said, "you don't need me to be successful."

"It's different."

"What's different?"

"This kind of success doesn't last."

"Neither does the other kind," I told her.

"I'd just have to close up my blouse."

"Please don't."

"If I don't, people will stop looking after an hour or two."

"I didn't know you were so modest."

"I've tried it already."

"Then show them something else."

"I want to be successful even when I'm not there. I want to make them dream."

"That's a bit harder."

"Not if you help me."

"You can't give success. You're either made for it or you're not."

"I know," she said with that challenging look I've come to expect. "I'm made for success, and I know I'll get it."

We walked past a giant Madonna poster. One arm raised, lips in a permanent pout, wooden cross nestling between her breasts. Metallic breasts. Madonna! The material girl is at the Stadium from the twelfth to the fifteenth. Every time Madonna comes to town, the mania for success reaches hysterical levels among sixteen- to twenty-five-year-old women. Erzulia kept her eyes from looking at the poster, but I saw that expression of pure hatred on her face.

PART FOUR

American
Chronicles

A Few Rules for Survival in America

1. Notes from the Underground: The New York Subway

Why is that young woman looking at me that way? What should I do about it? I can't very well ask her the time of day since my watch is showing. Nor can I talk about the weather, since we can't see outside. The slightest approach outside the strictly established rules would classify me as a wild-eyed rapist. The train rolls on as the young woman gazes upon me sadly, waiting for a sign from my quarter. Lucky for me, she has a book. Lord, make it be Hemingway, I have things to say about Hemingway. Oh, no, it's John Irving. What can anybody say about him? He's a big fan of honey, so it seems. I can't very well ask an intelligent-looking young woman what her sign is, this isn't the sixties any more. True, the custom dragged on into the mid-eighties, but welcome to the nineties, brother.

She's getting off at the next stop. She's taking her time about it, a lot of time, actually, looking through her purse for something, staring at the floor, then standing up. If she turns around and looks at me, she must really be interested. Other passengers are getting off, too. The car fills up again. New smells come in. The smell of people from Brooklyn and the Bronx mingles with the smell of people from Manhattan. The train moves off and picks up speed. I lose all hope. Suddenly, she turns around and what I see in her eyes makes me sick with despair. I can't believe that Western civilization, inventor of oral contraceptives, contact lenses, the telephone, the electric light, the theory of relativity and fast food, has still not been able to add one or two sentences to our very limited repertoire, a few words that would help an honest writer speak to a woman in the subway without frightening her. I can't believe no one has looked into the issue. One new sentence could change everything, a short sentence that wouldn't ask her the time, the temperature or her sign. What have two thousand years of civilization produced? Three unoriginal, ineffective ways of approaching a new woman. What poverty of imagination! Anyway, if a woman looks you in the eye in the New York subway, chances are she's a cop, a transvestite or a prostitute. Take your choice.

2. Chicago, State Street

I sit down on a bench to watch the human landscape. The Saturday afternoon crowds fill the streets. Why do I have the feeling that the same people keep walking by? They turn the corner, then reverse their steps. The same exhausted faces and twisted mouths. A crowd is normally composed of the same dozen people, multiplied by one hundred. Twelve types: the woman with two grocery bags that are too heavy for her, and make the veins on her neck stand out. The man in a hurry who's going nowhere. The girl who's just emerged from a department store. The happy child with an ice-cream cone that she's eating with her nose. The woman with her breasts bursting out of her blouse and her red mouth like a wound. A woman slapping a crying child. A young man pushing everyone aside because life isn't moving fast enough for him. A woman in her fifties walking slowly so she won't sweat. The tourist gawking at everyone and no one. A guy on a bike getting the evil eye. The child who stops to tie his shoes without telling his mother. A roving hand reaching out blindly and feeling up every pair of buttocks it can.

Watch out for that guy moving against the crowd, man. Check out his right hand. He's got a knife.

3. A Boston Restaurant

I took a table at the rear. It's hard to get a good spot in a restaurant when you're alone. I got out my notebook and started sketching out a few scenes, the portrait of the customers, some overheard bits of conversation, just to get into the swing of it.

Two white guys in tweed jackets came in.

"You go into a dining-room," one of them said to the other, "because that's what a restaurant is. You go into a dining-room, you sit down at a table that's already set as if they've been waiting for you, and right away someone comes up to serve you, they ask you politely what you want. You can answer

125

without looking at them, or you can let them know with just a pinch of irritation that you just got here and you want to catch your breath before making up your mind. The waiter'll say excuse me, then he'll go back to wherever waiters go and wait till you're good and ready to order something to eat, and meanwhile you inspect the menu, and when you figure you're in the mood to order, you motion to him and he comes galloping over. You place your order, he notes it all down politely, and if you change your mind, you start all over again, and he'll scratch out everything he's scribbled down. Then he'll ask you politely if that's all you want. You can tell him yes, or you can grunt something that might as well be in a foreign language. He won't think twice, he'll sprint off to the kitchen and a few minutes later, here he comes with a good hot meal. If the presentation or the cooking doesn't agree with you, you tell him you're disappointed, either gently or nastily, depending on how you feel. He'll tell you he's terribly sorry, no matter how you sounded, run back to the kitchen again and return a few minutes later with your food, this time perfectly presented. You look at him with a pitiless expression, and with a nod of your head let him know that it's okay, he can leave you to eat in peace now. He'll retreat, and he won't come back until he figures you've eaten all you're going to. Would you care for dessert? Since you didn't bother answering, he'll discreetly slip your bill under the ashtray and go back to his post, waiting until you're ready to call him over one last time to pay. Then you settle up, leave him a tip and head for the door."

"What's the point?" said the other man, after listening patiently to the whole monologue.

"Don't you think that's strange?"

126

"What's strange is having a waiter at your personal beck and call. Usually a waiter looks after more than one customer."

"It's a question of appearances, and that's not what I want to talk about. Don't you think it's strange that a total stranger would put himself at your service just for a few dollars? Meanwhile, that same person, outside of working hours, wouldn't do one-quarter of what he's just done for you, practically for free. He'd tell you to take a walk, even if you offered him ten times more."

"Working for one person is slavery, but when you do the same thing for a hundred different people, it's called work. The same waiter can get waited on in a different restaurant."

"The whole thing's understandable when the people are of the same group, or religion, or race. But look at this country: racial problems always begin in restaurants. The trouble begins when a white waitress has to serve a black customer when she feels she's superior to him."

"So you believe in apartheid?"

"At least it's not hypocritical."

"You're wrong."

I opened my ears wide. The conversation was beginning to get interesting.

"There's no such thing as hypocritical racism," said blue tweed to gray tweed. "There's racism—period. Racism becomes hypocritical when it has no other choice, when rules and laws try to block it. Or when the victims refuse to roll over and play dead. Then racism can't afford to show its true face; it puts on a veil. There's no such thing as racism that's ashamed of itself: if you're ashamed, already you're a little less racist."

The black waiter came gliding up.

127

"Care for a drink, gentlemen?"

Two obsequious faces looked up at him.

"Yes," said blue tweed.

"Of course," agreed gray tweed.

4. A Party in Beverly Hills

I was invited by the young African prince who's living with
Madonna. It's a rare event when Madonna throws a cocktail
party, and rarer still when Michael Jackson is seen out and
about. The entire world wants to talk to Madonna, but
Madonna only talks to Michael Jackson. Michael Jackson
doesn't even talk to God; his words are saved for children, animals and half-wits. Blessed are the poor of spirit, for the kingdom of God is theirs. Michael Jackson's kingdom of God is
Disneyworld. The evening got off to a slow start. People talked
about the number of records sold, who got gypped by whom,
who was bedding whom, who'd had the operation to change
sex, race, religion, nose, breasts, brain, orientation, persuasion,
lovers, or anything else you can do to get a new thrill.
Everyone chatted away until Michael Jackson showed up, followed by Madonna and the African prince. When Madonna
throws a cocktail party, she's always the last to arrive. Well, not
the absolute last; no one shows up anywhere later than Michael
Jackson. Madonna introduced the African prince to everyone.
Michael Jackson latched onto him and followed him everywhere. The caterer had done a marvelous job, but no one was
trying out his canapés—except the prince and I. The caterer
was catering to the prince, who was shoveling it in like a pig.

128

I told him he was eating too much.

"Too much is never enough," he said in a burst of laughter.

Here comes Warren Beatty, who'd spent the last hour in the bathroom with a young lady. Someone told me she was Drew Barrymore. Shirley MacLaine went by, and I heard someone say her guru had just quit her. A great peal of laughter rang out. "Who's that?" someone asked, munching on a carrot. The prince. Don't you know about Madonna's new lover? I heard she discovered him in some tiny village in North Africa. His grandparents were the last kings of Benin. He doesn't even know who Michael Jackson is. For him, America is Madonna, period. I hear he's a genius. What's he do? I told you, he's a genius. You'd have to be Madonna to grab the last authentic African prince. When she found him, he was dying in some thatched hut, covered with flies. The edifying story of Madonna and the African prince made the rounds that evening. Madonna was dazzling. The prince was eating. Michael Jackson introduced him to his monkey. The two of them recognized each other: old friends from the bush. People were circulating, and the party was starting to get interesting. But Madonna, Michael Jackson and the prince had already split. With the royal family gone, the subjects were free to fall upon the canapés, which they did with savage appetite.

I never saw the prince again, but the American papers got very interested in him. Television cameras came to film him sleeping. His sleep is positively post-Apocalyptic, a journalist from The *New Yorker* said. Madonna announced he'd be marrying her. Woody Allen was asked to film the wedding, but he turned down the assignment; too busy with his trial. Brian de Palma took the job. In *Rolling Stone,* Sean Penn announced he was going to change the prince's face around. Spike Lee declared that the prince wasn't doing the right thing. Why Madonna? he wondered out loud to The *Village Voice*; why not Queen Latifah? Queen Latifah piped up and announced that, in any case, she was a lesbian, and prince or no prince, she wasn't into men. Journalists called the prince. Stars called the prince. Shirley MacLaine called a couple of times. The prince never answers the phone. He's too busy eating or sleeping. Does he snore? Classified information. The *National Enquirer* confirmed that the prince was actually a white guy from Jersey fitted out in black skin. The only way, the reporter concluded, that this particular fan could get into Madonna's bed. That poses a technical problem: how is such a thing possible? It's not easy, the reporter wrote, but feasible if you have the money and determination that such a costly operation demands. You have to find a freshly deceased donor and get the family's permission. It's as simple as putting on a well-fitting suit, Calvin Klein chimed in. The operation is carried out in New York City, in the basement of a luxury Manhattan building. An anonymous source disclosed that Dr. Mengele was behind it, operating Mondays, Wednesdays and Saturdays, mornings only. The story was growing by leaps and bounds. A psychiatrist from Yale University, after analyzing his drawings, declared that the prince had the mental capacity of a five-year-old. Norman Mailer, in a brilliant but overly long article on the latest book by Professor Liebovitz in the book section of The *New York Times*, went off on a long digression to respond to the Yale psychiatrist. In Mailer's opinion, the intelligence of a five-year-old is certainly sufficient for anyone who covets the job of president of the United States. Once again, the black establishment did not appreciate Mailer's humor, and he had to specify that his attack was directed against the fact that our recent presidents (Ford, Reagan, Bush) were immature, irresponsible, cruel children, and that he was in no way suggesting anything negative about the mental capacity of blacks nor their ability to run the affairs of state. Unfortunately, Mailer had to add that the whole thing was so clear that even a child could understand it. This kind of declaration was hardly going to defuse the American racial time-bomb. An angry letter signed by twelve eminent black artists and intellectuals in The *New York Times* fanned the flames of the ancient racial fire. Do whites have the right to say anything about blacks, be it positive or negative? The answer was an unequivocal *No, never!* Mailer was in the middle of drawing up his vitriolic response, the major part of which was centered on the writer's freedom of expression (Mailer, as we all know, isn't afraid of anyone) when the rumor broke that Madonna had called it quits with the prince. All eyes turned to Madonna's new lover: the Dalai Lama. He'll do anything to attract the world's attention to his people's misfortunes, a *Los Angeles Times* editorialist commented with an irony not devoid of compassion. And what *she* wouldn't do to attract attention to herself, *Vanity Fair* retorted. Shirley MacLaine is going to die of jealousy, The *Village Voice* chortled. After all, she gave the Dalai Lama every penny she had.

Not long ago, I met up with the prince in Brooklyn, and he told me everything. He's no more prince than you or I. He comes from Port-au-Prince, and the city's name gave him the idea: if you were born in Port-au-Prince, you're just naturally a prince. He spent three years plotting his hoax, back when he was working in a laundry on Church Avenue. As a matter of fact, that's where I ran into him. In America, you always go back to the first job you ever had—don't forget that, brother.

5. Alabama in the Afternoon

An interracial couple is walking quietly through the streets of a Southern town. Is this love or provocation? Will the whites or the blacks attack them first? The bets are on.

The Great Black Hope

Sam, a young woman of my acquaintance, set up the meeting. Some kind of meeting! Spike didn't want to see me, and I felt the same way. Spike Lee had come to town, invited by the University of Miami, to speak about his work, his cinematic vision and all the terrible problems black filmmakers have to face in one of the most savagely racist societies on earth—you know, the usual bit. The problem is that Spike Lee is not the kind to take that lightly. I told the woman over and over that Spike Lee's version didn't interest me, that I'd heard it all before, that it was old stuff for me, that his vision of the world didn't inspire me and that there was no reason to share even a hamburger with a guy who insists on believing that America would have gone up in flames if he, Spike Lee, had been kept from making his film on Malcolm X. In the States, if a film is good, it will be shown in a dozen theaters (in other words, it won't be shown at all), but if it's bad, they'll put twenty-five million into advertising and show it in two thousand theaters. Either his film will be good, and we'll never see it; or it'll be bad, and I won't see it. Besides, I suspect Spike Lee wanted to make a film about himself making a film about Malcolm X. In other words, to make Malcolm speak for his own obsessions. But, as I said, Sam was putting pressure on both of us.

"Why should I see him, Sam?"

"No one can ignore Spike."

"Sorry, but I stopped counting on other people a long time ago."

"Now you're talking like him."

"Don't insult me!"

"Stop talking trash ... How about today?"

"All right, if I have to."

"You can't do a piece on America without talking to Spike Lee."

"Sam, I can do a piece on America without meeting anybody. Landscapes tell America's story better than anyone can. The only problem is that I hate nature."

"He's flying out this afternoon."

Sam must have had a world of trouble convincing an American star (even a black star; *especially* a black star) to meet a reticent nobody (even if that nobody was a contender for the title of greatest black writer alive). As far as Americans are concerned, if something isn't American, it might as well be ancient Hebrew. The Romans thought the same way when their city ruled the known world. The French followed that principle back when France could still bluff and deceive the rest of Europe. The Germans thought that way and still do. Sam must have told him I'm not one of his fans; maybe that's what convinced him. The rendez-vous was officially set, as if it were a boxing match, for a Miami Beach bar.

My first impression was of an angry child cursed with a

frail body. A Brooklyn Dodgers baseball cap jammed onto his frog head. Very beautiful eyes, and so gentle, too; his mother's eyes. Michael Jordan gym shoes on his feet and a *Do the Right Thing* T-shirt (a walking billboard). No rings on his fingers or diamonds in his teeth; he's a juvenile delinquent, not a pimp.

I went on the offensive immediately.

"So you're making a film about Malcolm X?"

"It's my right."

"Everybody has that right."

Anger shot out from his eyes.

"No, not everybody. That's why I'm making this film. I don't want some white man wrecking the story by turning it into a musical comedy with a happy ending."

"Funny you should say that. Listening to you, I'd almost think that whites had nothing to do with Malcolm, even though they were the very ones he wanted to blow away."

"Exactly my point. I didn't want Malcolm ending up co-opted by the very people he spent his life fighting."

"If it was up to me, I would have gotten a white to make this film. I'm sure a white would have gotten closer to the truth of Malcolm X than any black."

Spike Lee looked at Sam. Sam looked at the ceiling. I'm sure he must have been wondering whether I wasn't one of those provocateurs the FBI sics on you whenever you try to do something worthwhile in America. They did it with Martin; they did it with Malcolm. Nothing says they won't do it with Spike. Martin, Malcolm and Spike—a noble line.

"Why's that?" he asked anxiously.

He looked like a young boxer who'd just taken a savage blow below the belt while the referee had his back turned.

135

"Because a white would have been so afraid to screw up that he'd stick strictly to the facts. Imagine a white guy making a film about Malcolm X! First of all, he'd have to be pretty brave to face the anger of all those young blacks who think that Malcolm belongs just to them, not to the middle class or the black bourgeoisie, but just to them."

"You don't know anything about America. It's just mental masturbation. That's what whites have been doing for the last two hundred years: coldly eliminating a whole section of American history—*black* history."

"That's not the same thing. You can't boil everything down to—"

"It's the exactly same thing."

"Your own personal business, Spike, is not the same thing as the history of blacks in America."

"Nothing's changed!" Spike barked. "If they could, whites would lynch us all tomorrow morning."

"But they can't. Those are the facts; that's history. We can't act as though history didn't exist. Spike, they can't get away with a mass lynching of blacks in the United States any more. That reality counts. Our desires don't count, understand? Can whites lynch blacks in America? The answer is no. Would they like to be able to? The question doesn't exist. It has no meaning. What counts is what is, and what you do with it."

Spike Lee had gotten to his feet as I was shouting. He had his jacket in his hand.

"Ask him what he means, Spike," Sam interrupted. "You're not going to answer his question by running away."

Apparently, Sam had a certain influence over Spike Lee. Foaming at the mouth, in a cold rage, Spike sat down after a moment's hesitation. His right hand was trembling slightly.

"I'm tired of this struggle," I said. "We're wasting too much energy in constant struggle, valuable life energy. Creation is how I'm going to build my identity."

"Who wouldn't want the easier job?" Spike shot back. "But what can you do? There's a job, and I have to do it."

"Even if it means sacrificing your art."

"What are you talking about? Don't tell me you still believe in that white bullshit! I want to do things in the most effective way possible. I want to tell the truth, the truth about our past and our present. That's my job. It's a job I have to do because nothing has changed in this country."

"All right, let's say that whites haven't changed, though I'm not so sure about that. But what about blacks? They've changed. The proof is that you're making films. For a guy from the New York slums, you have to admit that—"

"You're missing the point, and no wonder: you're repeating word for word what the whites have been saying in every paper in this country. The same old song: *the country's changed*. I'd like to know how it's changed. Look at that young black man making movies in Hollywood, they tell us. As if I hadn't had to fight to make those films. No one ever gave me a break. They finance me because my films make money. I'm fighting to make films for blacks, by blacks and with blacks."

It was Spike's turn to lose his cool. Two screaming men, drunk with the need to shout out their truths. Sam seemed to be enjoying herself. That's what she'd hoped for, and that's what she'd gotten.

"I refuse," I said after a short truce, "to put people in the position where they can't tell me what they think of my work."

"What are you getting at?"

"That's what you do with your films. The white critics are afraid to say what they think of your work, afraid some mob in Brooklyn, Chicago or Los Angeles will lynch them. That's not art, that's street fighting."

"That's the way it is here, Daddy-O. This is America. If you don't like the heat, get out of the kitchen."

"It's artificial heat."

"Nobody in the USA is afraid to say what they think of my films. The whole thing's about power. The blacks are still weaker because they don't own the media."

"That's all anyone talks about in this country. The old refrain about power. Who controls who, the blacks or the whites."

"That's not my problem. I make movies; the rest doesn't interest me."

"They all say that."

Sam motioned to Spike, touching her watch. He had a plane to catch in less than two hours and two more interviews to do. Naturally, the airplane wouldn't wait for him.

"Of course," I said. "But I'm sure the plane would have waited for Warren Beatty, Robert de Niro or any third-rate politician."

"You see," Spike Lee said to me with a smile, "you can understand when you want to."

I gave him the last point. After all, the match was taking place on my home field, in Miami.

"If you come to New York," Spike told me as he slipped on his black leather jacket, "call me up, and we'll do round two."

The Skin Trade

The race issue has supported a lot more whites than blacks, though blacks have managed to survive on the crumbs. A lot of people wonder when it all began. When did one man look at another man and, surprised to notice the color of his skin, so different from his own, decide that he was his inferior? When you put this legitimate question to academics, who are normally crazy about details, and can tell you what happened millions of years before humans ever set foot on this earth, suddenly they get vague, unsure, even confused. "Oh, very far back in time" is the only answer anyone's been able to pry out of the researchers at the University of California at Berkeley, an institution at the forefront of the social sciences. The average person wants to have the exact date, if possible, an odd number. The question is straightforward and deserves our attention and should interest men of science. When did it all begin? Who saw the other one first? Who bellowed first, "You're not as good as I am?" The white or the black? The yellow or the red? The white or the yellow? The red or the yellow? The black or the red? The yellow or the black? The red or the white? I'm talking about the very first time, the critical moment when the eyes first met. Then I have another question, even more intriguing: when is it all going to stop? Is there an end? Or better yet, why is it all still continuing when ninety percent of people say they're against racism? Allow me to propose an answer to that question: money. People have a hard time believing that money is behind it, even though all the parties involved make a little something. Even the great writer James Baldwin sidesteps the money issue and offers a psychological hypothesis. In his opinion, the black is America's psychological basement; his very existence keeps the whites from hitting the bottom of the barrel. Every time a white man gets desperate in the USA, he knows there are people lower than he is, the true bottom dogs, the forest floor. Baldwin thinks that this is enough to reassure some people. The poorest, most desperate white man knows that millions of blacks envy his fate, and that helps him survive. Sorry, Baldwin, you're wrong. People never look down. The ground can't be a reference in the life of an individual. The social ladder is there to climb, and what counts is the next rung. No one looks down in search of consolation. Desperation comes from the prospect of all those rungs you have to climb to reach the summit, where the gods reside. No, Baldwin, the black man's situation doesn't help the white man, even psychologically. Economically, yes. In America, money provides reassurance. Money is a living thing. The Japanese call it "most honorable money". Money has a smell, a color, a taste, it can transmit harmful germs—though it's not contagious. Whites instituted racism for money, and the power that produces it. Malleable, tireless labor at rock-bottom prices: such was the black in white man's eyes. Let's trace back the tangled threads of American history. The song of American blacks. Racism created the American South, which created the blues, which gave new blood to show business. American showbiz brings in billions every year. It created Michael Jackson, an android who's neither black nor white, red nor yellow. Everyone hates Michael Jackson because he has achieved the impossible: he has transformed himself into a being with neither sex nor color nor race nor—given his privileged relationship with his monkey—identity, or so some people say. I'm not talking about racial or national identity or some such nonsense; I'm talking true, deep identity. Is he animal or human? I'm not on the side of blacks or whites or even monkeys, but between man and ape, is he the missing link? Or is he an incomplete black for blacks, an incomplete white for whites, an incomplete monkey for monkeys? All three categories share one common interest: music. And, music, brother, is worth millions. Sun Tzu in *The Art of War* said, "We loot the enemy because we lust after his wealth." Racism is undeclared war. Now we know why whites have refused to make this war official, it's one of the deadliest, cruelest, longest ones in history. Though admit it: it has done great things for the progress of Western civilization, a world that includes white, black and red—the yellows have stayed home. Whites have gotten rich off the gold mine called racism, so do you think that blacks, who have only just started living off racism after years of mistreatment, are going to accept the end of it? And just when they were starting to live off it? All those painters painting bodies twisting under the lash of the whip to sell to young whites right out of Northern liberal-arts colleges! All those musicians with all that rhythm singing

141

about the frustration of blacks in the urban jungle! All those moviemakers (starting with Spike Lee) using the big screen to portray the rage and violence of young black males in the powder-keg ghettos! What would I talk about if it weren't for the juicy, inflammable subjects of sex, race and money? Hear ye, hear ye, brothers, if there was no racism, American show business would fall apart tomorrow, and Japanese music would invade our airwaves! The racism issue puts liberal intellectuals on edge, but they should set aside their emotions. If we all agreed to make money off racism, nobody would have anything to complain about. We'd have it made in the worst of all possible worlds. The art of living in hell—business is business! We'd consider racism as one more natural resource, like a mine. But life isn't that simple: some guy has to make a video with a close-up of tears rolling down his cheeks and superimposed scenes of racial violence, real scenes where real blacks are getting beat up, while the guy in the foreground doesn't even have a scratch! It's all designed to lighten our pockets and make us pay to hear someone reeling off the litany of our suffering. To make matters worse, we're supposed to admire the guy, for he's a defender of the Race.

PART FIVE

The Hall of Fame

[Ten Contemporary American Heroes]

I

A Rap with Ice Cube

Ice Cube is probably the most listened-to rap artist in the United States. His first album, *Amerikka's Most Wanted*, influenced an entire generation of street poets. When Ice Cube speaks, the black ghetto listens. He just came out with his second album, *Death Certificate*, which is big news in the poor neighborhoods of all the big cities. He was twenty-three when I met him, shortly after the Los Angeles riots.

"I'm doing a piece on America, Ice."

"America? Which America?"

"The United States of America."

"The blacks' or the whites'?"

"Both."

"What do you want to know?"

"The heart of the matter."

"Master and slave."

"That's been around ..."

"Nothing's changed, man, everything's like before. Exactly

145

the way Abraham Lincoln found it."

"But—"

"We're living the way the white man always wanted us to. The master doesn't even have to be there any more. We've got his name, we dress like him, we dream like him, we eat like him, we think like him. Don't need to lock us up in the slave quarters any more at night, the ghetto does the job."

"That's funny. I didn't notice that black Americans ate and dressed and danced like white people."

"The youth is trying to do different, but they lack education, I mean, about their own roots. They're doing what they can to get by."

"There are other ways of seeing it, Ice. Blacks and whites have created a new culture together: contemporary America. Blacks may have influenced whites as much as the other way around."

"No. There aren't enough of us. Our culture isn't dominant. We don't act, we react. We don't control the media, we don't have our own police, we don't have schools where our values are taught, or not enough of them, we don't have our own industry, we don't have anything that might create this America you're talking about. Brainless blacks and white liberal intellectuals are circulating that kind of trash, but we've got nothing for ourselves down here."

"You mean airplanes, cars, hot water, bourbon, suits, electricity, Kentucky Fried Chicken, shoes, wristwatches, gold chains? You're going to let the whites have all that?"

"I try to consume as little as possible."

"Don't you think that's all part of universal culture?"

"That culture has made it to the top, and now it's imposing

146

its system on everyone else—that's how I see it."

"No matter where it comes from, anyone can help himself."

"We can't. Those aren't our ways, our tastes, our vision of life, man." He paused. "It was made with our blood and our sweat, brother, but against our will, and you can believe it."

"Are you against blacks who use the telephone?"

"No. But one day we'll build our own way of living. The white man invented all kinds of machines to make communication easier, but nobody is communicating with anybody else. In the days of slavery, blacks didn't have any telephones, but everybody knew what was happening on the other plantations, even ones that were miles away."

"Meanwhile, can blacks use the telephone, even if a white person invented it?"

"Yes, as long as they don't forget the other ways of communicating."

"Are you talking about spirituality?"

"That's exactly what I'm talking about."

"There's not much spirituality in rap. You sing about sex and violence and woman-hatred."

"No. We're trying to show the way you shouldn't go. It's another way of teaching. We do it with the language of youth. Our young people are desperate. Every day, the white police oppress them a little bit more. The ghetto is no playground."

"Sure, but aren't you afraid young people will take your songs literally?"

"They're not stupid."

"When I hear them repeating your songs, I get the feeling they like calling women bitches and glorifying violence."

"Rap is cool. We're trying to build a new school system, via TV. We're giving our young people something new. They've got to understand that what Uncle Sam teaches them is nothing but lies, it's not made for them. American culture was built against them, against us. All they want is to destroy us, to destroy every trace of our culture, our energy, our values."

"What about the Nation of Islam?"

"Yeah, the Nation of Islam, the Reverend Farrakan. He's the only black leader in America. The other leaders are followers. They don't even know they're white."

"Including Jesse Jackson?"

"Jesse Jackson, too."

"Your fight against white America has obsessed you to the point where you don't see anything else. Do you pay attention to what's going on in the rest of the world?"

"We're fighting the most powerful enemy in the world."

"Sure, but from the outside, you look like a typical American: rich, violent and arrogant."

"I've always seen myself as an African."

"That's not what the Africans would say."

"My place is in Africa."

"That's the Ku Klux Klan's opinion, too."

"Then I agree with the Klan on that point. Blacks belong in Africa."

"Do you believe in racial purity?"

"I believe we're at war."

"Listen, Ice, I've traveled all over the United States to write this piece, and I can tell you that the black ghetto is the most close-minded group of people on the face of the planet. You don't open up to anybody."

148

"Ghettos are barracks, and this is war."

"Tell me about the war."

"We're fighting on two fronts. Against the enemy and against what the enemy has made of us."

"And what has he made of you?"

"You said it yourself: the most close-minded group of people on Earth."

II

Billie Holiday: A Strange Fruit

I met Billie through Jim Monroe (no relation to Marilyn), her husband at the time.

She was getting out of a taxi in front of a bar (I don't remember if it was in Chicago or New York) when a man called out to me from inside the car.

"Hey, you, I'm Jim Monroe, Billie Holiday's husband. You want to help her cross the street? Look at her, she's completely stoned, and I'm not any better. We're talking Billie Holiday, son ..."

He dug around in his pockets in search of a few coins and seemed sincerely sorry that he couldn't find any.

"I don't have a penny, son. But you'll be able to say that you helped Billie Holiday cross the street one night when she was completely gone ... That'll be your way of exploiting her."

That evening, I helped Billie Holiday reach the far sidewalk.

Her body was heavy. Built for comfort. Hard inside, as if she carried a stone there. A strange fruit.

III

Miles Davis Plays Dolls

I knocked on Miles Davis' door. It looked like any other door. I heard noise from inside, like a mouse scratching. I knocked again. Finally, a little girl opened the door. She said something in a soft voice.

I had to lean over to hear her.

"He said to say 'fuck you.'"

"What?"

"That's what he said."

"Does he know who it is?"

"No. That's what I have to say every time someone knocks on the door."

"That's not a very nice word."

"I know."

"Then why do you say it?"

"Because he gives me a dolly."

"Every time?"

"Yes."

Then she gently closed the door again.

IV

Basquiat: O.D. on Success

I met Jean-Michel Basquiat a few days before he died. Before or after, it doesn't really matter. He was buying fruit at three o'clock in the morning. Oranges, I remember. I had seen one of his canvases by sheer luck at a Haitian friend's house in Brooklyn. It was like getting slugged in the gut.

"Who's that?"

"Basquiat. Don't you know Jean-Michel Basquiat?"

"I do now."

A single painting was enough to bring him into our lives. But who was Jean-Michel Basquiat?

I searched madly through my notebook.

Jean-Michel Basquiat, 1960-1988, black, drug addict, bisexual, Haitian (his father), Puerto Rican (his mother), street kid, entered the Whitney Museum of American Art.

The bourgeois art world was shocked. The first time that had happened since Jean Genet.

Basquiat was in the Whitney Museum, but Basquiat wasn't

152

there to enjoy it. A cocaine overdose.

Madonna's money made the show possible. Basquiat: a young Goya. New York subway. Graffiti. The end of the 1970s. In 1983, he met Andy Warhol. Basquiat wanted more than fifteen minutes of fame. He got it on February 10, 1985. A long article in *The New York Times*. A picture of Basquiat in a tuxedo, barefoot, with a look in his eyes like a young warrior who'd tear the throat out of anyone who'd stand between him and the sun. The title: "New Art, New Money: The Marketing of the American Artist."

It all came tumbling down on Friday, April 12, 1988. He was found dead in his Manhattan loft. At first, Basquiat was afraid he wouldn't last the standard fifteen minutes. In the end, he toughed it out three years. Like Jesus Christ, who also died on a Friday.

V

Magic Johnson

I was watching TV in my hotel room. I'd been in this one-horse Midwest town for three hours, and I figured I'd seen it all from my window.

The TV was across from the bed. In the old days, there used to be a Bible in every hotel room. The television replaced it. No one ever opened the Bible. You don't even have to turn off the TV when you check out. That's American democracy.

An unusual disturbance was coming from the television set. I turned to look at it. The handsome face of Magic Johnson, the most famous basketball player in the world, was glowing before my eyes, covered in sweat and forced smiles to announce he had contracted that terrible disease.

All America watched it with me. There are times like that on TV.

In twenty years, people will ask each other, "What were you doing when Magic Johnson announced he had AIDS on TV?"

I was in some nowhere little Midwest American town, sitting on my hands.

VI

Toni Morrison

I like Toni Morrison. I don't like her books. She would rather people like her books, even if it meant not liking her. I like Toni Morrison's books. The writer in question would rather we liked her more than her books. People are never satisfied. Ideally, we would like both Toni Morrison and her books. You can't have everything in this life. That's the first thing we learn, my dear Toni. The second is that we all have to die. Too few people remember those lessons.

Toni Morrison is a famous black American woman novelist who won the Pulitzer Prize. On the very next day, a photographer from *Newsweek* came to take her picture. An editor at the magazine confirmed that very afternoon that she'd be on the cover in a week or two. She waited eleven months.

"The week I was on the cover, you can bet nothing else important was happening in the world."

Just for once, it would have been nice if something (an assassination, a war, a coup) had happened somewhere in the world.

VII

Derek Walcott

Here comes Derek Walcott.

Walcott, Nobel Prize for Literature, 1992, was born in 1930 in Saint Lucia, a small island in the West Indies. These days, he's teaching at some American university.

The morning the Prize was announced, the American press descended *en masse* on Walcott's place, to no avail: the little apartment he had lived in over the last few years was empty.

Derek Walcott was having his breakfast in a short-order joint just downstairs. He greeted the press in his slippers and seemed quite surprised to have received the Nobel Prize for a handful of poems on the island fishermen and daily life in this former Dutch colony. The photo of the Nobel laureate sitting in front of a cup of smoking coffee was seen the world over.

With the one simple, humble gesture, Derek Walcott became an American hero.

I like Derek Walcott. And I like his books, too.

VIII

Naomi Campbell

Naomi posed for photos with Madonna. Naomi kissed Mike Tyson in a restaurant washroom in Manhattan (it was raining that evening). Naomi was photographed by Avedon. Naomi left Cindy Crawford's party early last night. Naomi had a secret rendez-vous with Prince. Naomi went bike-riding with Mick Jagger in Central Park. Naomi knew Jackie Kennedy. Naomi lives in Los Angeles with Robert de Niro. Naomi works for Revlon. Naomi flies to Paris more often than a stewardess. Naomi turned down a role in the last Spike Lee picture. Naomi fought off Arnold Schwarzenegger and thought nothing of it. Naomi doesn't like to show her breasts. Naomi reads before turning off the light. Naomi loves Dashiell Hammett novels. Naomi won't watch anything but old films on TV. Naomi would like to be Ingrid Bergman. Naomi thinks Onassis would be more seductive if he weren't so rich. Naomi doesn't like the Italian type. Naomi eats spaghetti every day. Naomi's never been to Africa. Naomi hates being called the black Bardot.

I carry Naomi's pictures with me wherever I go. As soon as I check into a hotel room, I pin them to the wall.

IX

Rodney King

One night, Rodney King, a black man, was arrested by white policemen in Los Angeles.

From his window, a man filmed the entire scene. Rodney King was beaten up by a half-dozen white officers. An all-white jury acquitted the policemen. Furious, the blacks burned the city down. The American judicial system retried the policemen some time later and managed to convict two of the four charged. America split the deal fifty-fifty.

Every black American family went out and bought a camcorder. Nowadays, as soon as the police get out of their cars in a black neighborhood, folks reach for their cameras.

X

James Baldwin: A Portrait

James Baldwin's the one I want to talk to. As you know, Baldwin is dead, Baldwin, the most honest of men. The only writer I can fully trust. Every time I lose faith in the human kind, I open one of his books and discover the most acute intelligence combined with the finest sensitivity. Baldwin is a man after my own heart. I'm sitting at the window in this Harlem apartment, at the poet Quincy Troupe's place, not far from where Baldwin spent his childhood and adolescence as the pious son of a pastor. The narrow street is empty. A few stunted trees in the park. From time to time, a siren screams. Men have always preferred to die at dawn, a gentle hour for a violent death. I like to think that those who wish to communicate with us also prefer that hour.

"Is it hard?"

Baldwin's particular voice. He sits down across from me. His ugly-duckling face hasn't changed. I glance down at his hands; a mandarin's hands, the kind Miles Davis had. Two great craftsmen. I try to compare the guy sitting across from me with the dozens of photos of Baldwin I saw in the little room Quincy Troupe uses as his office. I spent the whole night looking at them. Baldwin, at the time of his meeting with the novelist Richard Wright. There's Wright's round, almost child-like face, and next to him a frail young man in a black suit, already devoured by insecurity, a voracious reader, curious about everything, all exposed nerves, emotionally unstable. Baldwin dreamed of writing, and at the time Wright was the only black model for an ambitious young man. The only truly useful model for this strange young man with the sarcastic laughter who wanted to make that distinctive voice of his heard. His, the purest song: to become the greatest American writer. Wright was lifted to mythic stature after *Native Son*. Look at Baldwin's starving monkey face compared to the pow-erful build of the current title holder. You want to bet five to one on the challenger. Baldwin, the little guy, is a tough cus-tomer. From their very first meeting, he was already plotting to devour the father (poor Wright!). Baldwin in Paris, all skin and bones, penniless, raging, writing by night, idling away the days. A Negro was freer in Paris—freer to starve. But the wine cost next to nothing and the cafés never closed. He would go from bar to bar, hitting on his few friends for a drink, picking up the tips left by over-generous customers. Baldwin, writing in an unheated room, talking with Chester Himes at the Café de Flore, gazing at Camus from a distance; Camus, the North African, Baldwin, the Negro. Baldwin returning alone to a meager supper in his attic room with space enough for a bed and a typewriter and not much more. Except for books, and they're everywhere: on the bed, under the bed, on the table,

162

under the table. In this hovel, he prepared his attack on white America. First, a stern warning, then the fire next time. Baldwin strolling down the Champs-Elysées of an afternoon. He saw the headline: *America in Flames.* So soon! The terrified face of the young black man entering a school that until then had been the private domain of whites, in the American South. His last day in Paris. Baldwin, in a Greyhound bus driving into the deep South. Baldwin, deep in discussion with Martin Luther King, in a parking lot with Medgar Evers, with Bayard Ruskin in Birmingham, shortly after the church bombing. Baldwin on TV after the publication of his devastating essay, *The Fire Next Time* (the Biblical warning). Baldwin typing out those fiery words that would fly off the paper and strike the enemy in the heart. Baldwin, a man of the heart, the man who wanted to understand America in the heat of the 1960s, the man whom both blacks and whites took turns hating. Baldwin who offered his serene, lucid light as contrast to the twilight of blood that racists on all sides called for and will continue to summon down with all their fervor. Baldwin, the preacher's son who put the furious eloquence of black religion into the racial balance as a way of facing the worst racial hatred: that of young whites in the American South. Baldwin was bent on shaking old Faulkner out of his perverse nostalgia. Faulkner, the gentleman-farmer, who yearned for the long trails of slaves in the cotton fields of Mississippi, who still dreamed of black women bent over cotton flowers. Baldwin, desperate, at his patience's end, announcing the coming fire one final time.

And the fire did come.

James Baldwin considered me with his wide, glaucous

163

eyes. He was on the other side now, and he looked relaxed about it. After a couple minutes, I finally recovered the faculty of speech.

"Above all, it's long."

Baldwin looked at me and smiled gently, as if removed from all concern.

"Time doesn't exist."

"Come on, Jimmy. Even for a dead man, that must be a cliché."

"Don't say that. It's the only truth that really counts."

"You can be sure time exists for those of us who have to suffer death."

"We don't die, man."

"Listen, Jimmy, I don't want to debate time with you. It wouldn't be a fair fight."

"What do you want to talk about?"

"Racism. What else?"

Baldwin's face became so sad I wanted to reach out and take his hand.

"Let me give you a piece of advice," he said to me in an even voice. "Forget about racism, it's not your business. It'll burn the heart right out of you. We're better off leaving racism to the racists. It's a sickness, and they have to try and wipe it off the face of the planet themselves. You can't be both the sickness and the cure. Don't worry about it. If you do, you won't have time for anything else."

"What do you mean?"

"It used to be our problem back in the old days. Our racism problems monopolized everyone's attention, and no one else, and nothing else, could occupy any space. It was our problem,

164

and no one else had the right to get involved. Nowadays, I think we should leave other people the opportunity."

"Even racists?"

"Why not? If you leave them a little space, they'll feel like they're part of things. Whites absolutely have to get involved in racism, too."

"Blacks didn't invent racism, Jimmy! I know they're paranoid, but they're not that bad!"

"That's my opinion on the subject, and now you know it."

"Don't get mad ... What about homosexuality?"

"What about it? Homosexuality is my business. It's a private affair."

"Of course, Jimmy, but what's it like now?"

A burst of high-pitched laughter.

"Don't go imagining things. We still have desires but, naturally, no erections."

"How come? Why do we still have left-over desires?"

"It seems I didn't work out all my fantasies when I was on Earth. It's a kind of first level, or so they say. I have no idea, really ..."

"Excuse me for going back to it, but is there any discrimination where you are?"

"Racial? No."

"What about sexual? Is there any lust in heaven?"

Jimmy slapped his thigh (I heard nothing) and gave a hearty black laugh.

"Not as far as I can tell."

"But you could have a sexual relation with an angel if the opportunity presented itself."

"I suppose so. Except for the erection problem, as I

mentioned."

We considered the question in silence.

"So what are the chances, Jimmy?"

"Well, besides the little detail about not having any erections, I suppose it would be possible to score an angel."

"Should I deduce that it hasn't happened yet?"

"No, not yet."

Suddenly Baldwin seemed to find the proceedings hilarious.

"So, then, everything's okay. No racism, no sexual discrimination, it's cool up there."

Baldwin's face darkened (a metaphor, of course).

"Well, sort of ..."

"What's the problem, Jimmy?"

"There are hardly any blacks up here."

"That's funny. Since they go through hell on earth, I would have thought there'd be plenty in heaven. So they're lying to us on that account, too!"

"I heard they decided to choose hell. I guess they felt more comfortable with the familiar," Baldwin sighed with his world-weary smile. "There's no use complaining ... I've got Chester here, but Richard was moved up to a higher level not too long ago. Good old Wright, always near the seat of power!"

"Do you talk about literature?"

"I feel a little removed from all that."

"Then what do you do all day, if you don't mind me dividing eternity into little squares?"

"We sing."

"That's a terrible cliché!"

"Sorry, it's true ... We blacks have got a leg up. The Boss loves to hear us sing. And remember, I'm a preacher's son."

166

"Still, I can't believe it."

Baldwin began to fidget on his chair.

"I don't have much time left. What do you want to know? And make it snappy."

"Since you have so much time for contemplation, what do you think about the life you led down here?"

"It was absurd. I was born in the wrong century, at the wrong place, I had the wrong color and the wrong sex. But I have no regrets."

"Masochist!"

"Quick, your next question."

Baldwin's shadow began to fade.

"How can I be a good writer for the 1990s?"

"What does that mean?"

"A writer of my time."

"I was a writer of my time, too, and look what happened to me ..."

"What happened, Jimmy?" I asked frantically.

"I grew more and more invisible."

He was right. There was nothing left but his smile.

PART SIX

America Is a Giant TV Set Full of Pictures Inside

Why Baseball Is America's Pastime

I was sitting at a table at the back of a crummy restaurant, minding my own business. I got the feeling the waitress was giving me the eye. A woman of mature years, slightly stooped, with bags under her eyes. She put down a tall glass of water on my table. Her hands were crisscrossed with thick blue veins, like a network of expressways leaving a major city. Her skin was so transparent I could almost see the blood moving through her body. A pair of hands that had washed a lot of dishes in thirty years. Two bitter wrinkles at the edge of her mouth gave a hint of her vision of the world. But when our eyes met, she was transformed into a blushing teenager. It didn't seem as though she had much to do today. Now and again, she glanced in my direction. An ancient sadness lay behind her gaze, the look of a professional waitress. A guy turned on the TV. Immediately, big, strong-looking guys started to charge across a field like beasts. Black and white; no Asians or women. Baseball is an essentially North American game. What's funny in the United States is that the past is so close you don't get any perspective on it. Everything happens on the same plane, like in folk art. In every movement that any American makes, all America can be found. Watch those guys strutting across the field and you'll see that baseball is a profoundly homosexual game. America is an essentially homosexual nation. I'm not talking about decadence and orgies; I'm referring to power. There's a sexual impulse behind this desire to dominate every other human being on the planet. Observe those handsome men with their aggressive buttocks displaying themselves on the field; here is a sport played by men for men. Baseball should be played naked. Instinct, ground, this feline grace—look at that guy on the screen. How slow his movements, how graceful. Then, suddenly, the action erupts in a fraction of a second: the beasts pounce. Southern afternoon, desire, bodies, water, the ritual dance. The same movements, reaching infinity. The pain that contorts the face, the invisible signs of fatigue, the studied casualness of the mouth, the alert eye. Suddenly, the sprint. Long, powerful, graceful legs. The player throws himself head-long into the dirt at the foot of the other player who catches the ball. Sacrificing the body. Abandonment, relaxation, exactly like an orgasm.

Why did the waitress give me that endlessly sad look as I walked out the door of the restaurant?

Why Did that Fat American Black Lady Kiss the Queen of England, and Why Did the Queen Smile?

If you want to discover America, you have to watch TV during the baseball season. When there's a game on, one third of American males (the percentage of women is negligible, except for a few West Coast intellectuals) are busy watching TV, the second third is listening to the radio because they're stuck in a traffic jam on a bridge somewhere, and the last third doesn't even need to listen to the radio or watch TV to know what's going on in the game. All American men are required to love baseball. Some women who still love men watch the game to keep up with the news. Most American women hate the sport for obvious reasons. Very quickly, they understand it's a secret ceremony with its rituals, sacred chants, high priests and millions of believers. Baseball is the American church with the greatest number of faithful. Followers must adopt a relaxed position (feet on a table, for example); obscene commentary is also highly recommended, especially after a superbly executed or scandalously muffed play. If your team

173

loses, it's normal to slap your wife around after the ninth inning. If a woman dared call the police to complain, she'd most likely end up listening to a heated discussion between her violent husband and the policemen she summoned about their team's missed opportunities. A policeman feels closer to the criminal who admires the same player than to the victim who doesn't share his passion. The fraternity of the diamond is stronger than law. Television announcers almost never break into a game, even for an earth-shattering announcement. Even if the end of the world were nigh, baseball fans would want to know when it was due, so they could get their game in before the Apocalypse. We'll see later; one thing at a time. Well, brother, believe it or not, today's game was momentarily pre-empted to show footage of the Queen of England's visit to North America. Most true fans in the small towns didn't even know the event was taking place until they turned on their sets this very day to watch Good Morning America. Despite every precaution, a great hue and cry of pain and astonishment went up just as the game was briefly pre-empted. Someone had committed the unspeakable: the world's most powerful men had been interrupted in the pursuit of their favorite game. There was a giant close-up of the Queen with her baby face, white gloves, inevitable hat and infinitely artificial sweetness. "Who's that lady?" grumbled a guy from Nebraska who hadn't been watching his set lately. Now the Queen was being filmed at a baseball game. She admitted that this was the first time she'd seen such a sport. All America smiled. She's naive, childish, likable—but enough's enough, let's get back to the game. Hold your horses! Now the Queen is visiting a battered-women's shelter. "What's that?" a guy from Alabama wanted

174

to know. That was how the heart of America discovered the existence of the problem. "What are they complaining about?" a guy from New Jersey hollered. "Let's get back to the game!" Suddenly, an enormous black lady filled the screen. All three hundred pounds of her bore down on the Queen and actually kissed her on both cheeks! Time stood still. "My name is Gwendolyn, but they call me Dolly." The Queen answered, "My name is Elizabeth, and they call me Lilibeth." Dolly's overture to Lilibeth was so perfectly human that the Queen couldn't help but feel a wave of pleasure travel up her spine and bloom on her face like a smile.

The coverage of the game resumed, but the world had changed. Since President Kennedy's assassination on live TV, no one had ever seen such a thing on the small screen.

PART SEVEN

Coming Home

Brother Monkey

Good old Bouba! Whatever happened to him? I haven't seen the face of the great hairy-headed American monkey for nearly eight years now. I remember the last time I saw him: he was moving slowly down the street, his back slightly bent, walking into the sunset. A drugged sun was staggering at the end of the block. I was with a woman I'd just met in a bar not far from there. Bouba kept on walking the other way, not hurrying, and the woman was pulling on my arm, wanting to know who he was. Eight years later, here he comes again, from the opposite direction, as if we'd never gone our separate ways, as if he'd just stepped out to buy something at the corner, and now he was coming back, his shirt sleeves hanging to his knees. Here he comes, a migratory bird unaccustomed to the ground, awkwardly sidestepping the cars, looking as though he were floating a few inches from the pavement. It's great to see that half-crazed hermit again, a guy who's completely oblivious and happy about it. Bouba goes strolling through the streets, whistling to himself, unconcerned with time, ignoring the outside world, not even thinking of himself, exactly the way I left him in the middle of the 1980s. As for me, the 1980s ran over me like a freight train.

I remember my last conversation with him. In his opinion, the novel I was finishing was going to make me famous. I was going to have to perform my duties as a famous writer by drinking great quantities of the finest wine, plucking the sweetest, blondest fruit from the tree of pleasure (the kind you see on the covers of fashion magazines), going to the theater, making movies, giving my opinions on the issues of the day, mingling with the privileged youth of America the Rich.

"That's why you worked as hard as you did, man."

As I walked out the door, I turned and saw that glow of mischief in Bouba's eyes. Gently, I closed the door and found myself on the sidewalk, my manuscript under my arm.

And now I'm back again. There's no shame in returning home if you do it to save your skin. I won't go any further into the issue. Right now, what interests me is Bouba as he dances through the cars that honk away at this African lost in the big city. I believe that Bouba created this city with his aristocratic hands, and each day he breathes life into it. He looks after it better than anyone else because he's so alive, more alive than all those other people who appear so energetic but only want to add to the city's daily madness. Bouba is the beating heart of this damned town, and it doesn't even know it. It would discover that fact only if the heart ever stopped beating. Now he sees me. He moves towards me without changing his step or speed, but the educated eye can easily distinguish the slight twitch at femur level, the small contraction of the stomach and an imperceptible tremor of the back muscles. All of which pitch him forward, as if his body were in free fall for a second

180

or two. The energy he expends to right himself reminds me of a young basketball player who had impressed me one afternoon in Brooklyn. When he's ten yards away, he stretches out his thin arms in my direction. A car screeches past, the driver accelerating hard. Bouba sucks in his stomach and rises on pointe, as if Nureyev had come to our streets to dance. A Nureyev who spits on social niceties, a living, fire-breathing Nureyev, the hungry young man from Russia, and not that poor devil executing entrechats for the pleasure of the heavy-breathing bourgeoisie snoring away in the loges of the Western world. Our Nureyev's body is covered with scars, for he has risked his life in the streets, the only stage where the danger is real. Another car cuts its way through the warm, early afternoon air. Bouba loses his balance and drops his bag of groceries trying to fight off the inevitable fall. Potatoes spill out on the burning asphalt. The soft thud of wheels crushing vegetables. Some cars try to avoid the well-tied bundles of carrots, while the eggplant and lettuce slip underneath the wheels. Bouba looks once behind him, then rushes into my arms. The cars zip by. Everyone is hurrying to their watering-hole for happy hour so they can get high before returning home to their conjugal hell. I feel Bouba's breath on my neck and his body in my arms. This is the drunkenness of euphoria: I am with the only guy I want to be with in all of America. I breathe in deeply. The trees and houses and cars and street are no more than a huge backdrop built for our reunion. Now that Bouba is here, we can strike the set.

Bouba's Endless Laughter in the Night

Bouba had been sitting in the darkness for a while now. When I came in, I recognized his shape on the old couch. His eyes wide open like an ancient monk's. The cool night air blew in through the window, and there I took my place.

People were going by below. A child ran after a yellow ball. An old couple. A car going too fast. The different rhythms of which life is constituted.

"That feels good."

"I'm glad."

"I hadn't done that for a long time."

"What?"

"Just sit by a window."

"I can understand that."

I'm not the guy walking in the street any more; I'm the one watching the others go by. I needed that respite.

"How was it?" Bouba asked abruptly.

"How was what?"

"Success."

"Fine."

"Failure's even better," Bouba chortled in the shadows.

Bouba brought his legs up to his chest in his preferred position: the fetal one. His spherical form created a mass denser than that of the earth. Bouba is like an ancient animal, lurking in darkness, motionless. Ignorant of time and the order of things.

An ambulance siren. Someone was fading fast. The Western world refuses to recognize death. We try to hang on. We invent new tools to fight boredom. War, work, travel, success, failure, schemes, the Mafia, important meetings, cars, TV, power, money, scientific breakthroughs, literature, cinema, skiing, everything you can find in the American surprise package.

"What remains, Bouba?"

Bouba's endless laughter shook the room. The laughter of a dancing god; the true voice of a man.

The Red-Eyed Goddess

Someone knocked at the door.

"Hello!"

Erzulia was pacing through the gentle shadows of the room. Bouba was sitting on the couch, calmly drinking his Shanghai tea.

"What the hell are you doing here?" she asked me.

"Nothing … I'm doing a story for an American magazine."

She looked at me suspiciously.

"What are you going to talk about?"

"It's vaguely about America."

"What's my part in it?"

"None. Why?"

"You promised me you'd write something!"

"I didn't promise you anything. I can't even promise myself anything."

"I'm not talking about you."

She looked me in the eye.

"You're a real bastard, you know."

"Listen, we're not going to start that all over again. I don't know you well enough. I don't know your habits, your secrets, your vision of life, your type of man, the way you sleep, your dreams, your desires ..."

Slowly, she started taking off her clothes. It's a regular compulsion with her.

"If that's what you wanted, why didn't you say so? Why waste time bullshitting? In a minute or two you'll have all the information you need."

Honestly, I'd never seen more beautiful breasts.

"I'll scratch yours, you'll scratch mine."

Lord in Heaven, what a perfect mortal coil!

"That's not what I was talking about," I stammered.

She was already naked, a true goddess of fire. The package was complete, and there wasn't a part too many. I feared for the limits of my being.

Someone cleared his throat. She wheeled around, and there was Bouba, on the couch.

"What's he doing there?" she spat.

"That's Bouba. We're at his place."

"You think I care? Can't he see we're busy, or is he blind?"

Bouba smiled beatifically.

"What's the matter with him? Is he retarded?"

"I don't think so," I said.

Bouba's smile widened.

"He must be a voyeur! I hate perverts!"

"Bouba doesn't even see you."

"A queer! I should have known—you're both queers!"

"He's just a man sitting quietly in his own house."

She threw her clothes back on and stormed down the stairway.

185

The King's Scribe

Bouba went out to buy food. I stayed behind by the window. That's been my only activity lately: watching people go by in the street. I know most of them by now. That little boy crossing the street with a long loaf of bread under his arm lives three houses down. That girl is a prostitute. I saw her once in the red-light district. The soldiers America is sending to the front are getting younger and younger; usually, that means the war is coming to an end. Whoever is down there hasn't bothered to knock; he's all but battering down the door. I opened it instead, and there was the Nigerian taxi driver.

"I was going by and I saw you at the window."

He sat down in Baldwin's chair, stared at me in silence, then got up again. He must have ants in his pants; he can't sit still for more than a few seconds. Then why did he choose a job where he has to be in a taxi all day long? Maybe he didn't choose it. Mind you, at least in a taxi, you move, the view is always changing, and the people are, too. But he and his routine never change. He's always raging in his army-surplus outfit. Any moment now, I expect him to pull a grenade from one

186

of those deep pockets.

Instead, he produced a heavy package all tied up with string and threw it on the table.

"What's that?"

He offered no reply.

"What I am supposed to do with it?"

His face was blank. I went to the table and took a closer look. It was a historical novel. I should have known. It must be more than a thousand pages long, some of it typed, the rest handwritten, with grease stains throughout. A barrage of odors assaulted my nose. He must have written this thing at the dinner table. No one can overestimate the role of canned spaghetti in black literature. I glanced at the Nigerian and discovered he had fallen asleep, so I decided to try to decipher this mishmash. If I understood correctly, it was the story of the last African kingdom at the height of its glory, that is, before the white devils showed up. Perfect harmony reigned. The author described every house, every plant, every inhabitant in the kingdom. The thing went on forever, and of course everything was perfect. "Evil" and "ugliness" didn't put in an appearance until the last chapters, in the person of the "white dogs". At that point, the author abandoned the ethnographic tone of the first two-thirds and took on a more direct style, something like a pamphlet. In other words, rage gained the upper hand. Insults poured from his lips. There weren't enough words to describe the Western dogs, but he did do his best. Sheets of pages, what a barrage! He never tired of spitting in the white man's face. By the way, it was also the best part of the book because finally he was truly himself, having dropped all scientific pretensions. He became a raging fire, he refused to accept those barbarians

187

destroying such a perfect kingdom and such a brilliant court. He hit his speed and nothing could stop him, not even the most basic rules of the novel, rules which he gladly accepted for the first two-thirds of the book. He set the novel during the final battle that would end with the defeat of his people. The king's army was in retreat, and the king himself in grave danger. This historic battle would preface the fall of the greatest African kingdom ever. The Nigerian described the battle just as the king, surrounded on all fronts, retreated into his private chambers, surrounded by his faithful guard. A white officer was preparing to smoke the king out of his chambers, or so goes the legend. But suddenly the author stilled the hand of the arsonist by blowing out his brains with his Magnum .357. The officer's astonished expression will go down in history, and researchers will puzzle over the mystery of where this strangely dressed, efficiently armed warrior came from. From that moment onward, the battle took a new turn. The Nigerian started handing out machine guns, Magnum .357s and even flame-throwers to the Mandingo warriors, who themselves were a bit surprised by this turnaround. "Who is this unknown warrior?" the king's guards asked each other. Who else but Ogun, God of Fire. "Ogun is with us, so let's exterminate the white dogs!" The king's army drove the white dogs into the sea. That's the way, the Nigerian concluded, that true patriotic historians should write history. Gone are the days of the impartial historian who watches the course of events and describes the extermination of his people without so much as lifting a finger. The author went on snoring, his head on the table. What was the king's scribe doing in this American inferno? He has come to spread the good news of a free kingdom and an indomitable king.

The King Was a Queen

Someone came crashing through the door; that seems to be the preferred way of entering my apartment. Erzulia advanced on me.

"Did you finish?"

"Finish what?"

"Shit! Did you finish writing my part or not?"

"Again? You're persecuting me!"

"What's that?" Erzulia asked with a look at the thick manuscript.

"It belongs to him. I haven't written anything."

Erzulia leaped on me and tried to grab the Nigerian's manuscript. I sidestepped her charge, but she ended up seizing the manuscript and throwing the pages all over the room. The Nigerian woke up.

"What's going on?" he wondered groggily.

Then his eyes opened as wide as saucers; he had understood. Erzulia's hysterical laughter rang out. The Nigerian ran every which way, trying to catch the pages landing in various places around the room. One page made it to freedom through the open window and flew heavenward. The Nigerian tried to jump out the window after it, but I grabbed him by the waist. Erzulia collapsed on the floor in endless, high-pitched howls of laughter. The Nigerian rushed down the stairs and snatched the wayward sheet of paper from under the wheels of a moving truck. Erzulia got up off the floor and ran into the bathroom. The Nigerian returned, out of breath but radiant. He sank into Baldwin's chair.

Erzulia emerged from the bathroom, naked. What did nudity mean to her? Nothing, apparently.

"What are you two cooking up?"

My senses sprang to attention. My eyes caressed the brush of down between her thighs. The Nigerian didn't seem to respond to that kind of thing.

"What are you writing about?" Erzulia demanded, moving in on him.

The Nigerian made a move to shield his manuscript under his arm.

"It's private."

"I don't know the meaning of the word," Erzulia informed him.

Indeed, she didn't.

"Show it to me."

"No."

The Nigerian retreated every so slightly. Erzulia's pudenda was lined up perfectly with his mouth. Just where it should be, brother.

"Give it to me."

The Nigerian held out.

Erzulia moved a little closer. Her pubic hair grazed his

lips. All was silent. A ray of sunlight sliced the room in two. The duel seemed to go on forever. The Nigerian kept his eyes on hers. Finally, she sat down on him.

"Tell me your story."

"It's too long," the Nigerian stammered.

I went out for a breath of fresh air; after all, I knew all about the chronicle of the forbidden kingdom.

In the stairway, I heard Erzulia scream, "Shit! He's not a king, he's a queen!"

I've Given Up Being a Black Writer

The same girl approached me on the street again.

"Are you still writing?"

"A little ..."

"Enough?"

"No. You've got to write a lot to get a little."

"In that case," she said with a sad smile, "you must not be left with very much at all."

"A portrait of Baldwin, a few short scenes, some lines of dialogue ..."

"That's all?"

"I'm afraid so."

"Is there anything you can do?"

"No."

"You seemed more enthusiastic the first time."

"I hadn't written anything yet. Writing's like making love: the best part is right before."

"Never during?"

"Sometimes. Sometimes in the morning."

"Why the morning?"

"Because I'm a morning person. You have to choose. Since I make love at night, I write in the morning."

She burst out laughing.

"Are you all that way?"

"Who are you talking about?"

"Writers," she said with a quarter-smile.

"I don't know. I don't associate with them."

"I thought writers hung out together."

"When I started writing, I promised myself two things. First: I'd never try to impose my stuff on other people. I hate people who invite you to their house for a drink then, fifteen minutes later, start reading their whole novel to you."

"Didn't you ever do that?" she asked skeptically.

"No."

"But that's what you do with the reader."

"That's not the same thing. The reader spends money on a book, and he'll read it when he's good and ready to."

"So you think the reader is free."

"Yes."

"And the junkie is free to buy his hit of heroin," she answered sarcastically.

"Reading isn't illegal."

She thought about that.

"Okay. What's the second thing?"

"That I'd never belong to any group. Groups are a waste of time."

"But I like seeing writers in cafés, watching them talk about their novels, listening to them read their poems with a glass in their hands until two o'clock in the morning."

"That's a nice image, but that's not how you write. Of

course, people can do whatever they want to. The few times I participated in evenings like that, it was like lying down in a nest of snakes. Hatred, envy and jealousy mixed in nicely with the wine and the laughter."

"Why do you have such a black view of life?"

She clapped her hand over her mouth, like a child who's just revealed a secret she had promised not to tell.

"I'm not blacker than anyone else. I'm just trying to see things as they are."

"And how are they?"

A quarter-second elapsed.

"They're black."

She laughed a healthy laugh.

"I like it when you get your sense of humor back."

"You like it when I lie. That's what humor is for: to hide your suffering."

"Good Lord, you're starting to take yourself seriously!"

"I think there comes a time in a man's life when he's got to say what's on his mind."

She reached up and stroked my forehead, a touch that would have been out of bounds if it weren't for my outrageously melodramatic tone.

"And what's on your mind?"

"Nothing, as it turns out."

"Aren't you exaggerating?"

"I thought I was filled with righteous anger, I thought it penetrated me to my very soul."

She looked a little lost.

"What's this 'it' you're talking about?"

"You know, the hatred of racism, of stupidity, of intolerance, everything that makes our century what it is ... and every other century, for that matter."

"And so?"

"It turns out those were just words. I'm totally unconcerned with the fate of blacks—or of anyone else, for that matter."

Her laugh was slightly ironic.

"That's what happens when you choose isolation and ignore your contemporaries. If you'd been out a little, you'd know that most people think the way you do."

I looked her in the eye.

"I know what they're like."

"So?"

"I was vain enough to think I was different."

"What gave you that idea?"

"I cherished the impossible dream of being equally hated by blacks and whites."

"Just so people would pay attention to you."

"Don't think that. I wanted to do something different from everybody else."

"Sure, but ..."

"Just about every writer I know is defending one cause or another: a race, color, religion, community or country. They're all lined up, ready for battle, but I wanted to step out of line."

"You certainly didn't try to duck out of the racial debate by writing *How to Make Love to a Negro*," she pointed out.

"You don't understand. I didn't say I didn't want to inquire into issues of race; I just wanted to do it in a non-propaganda way. I wanted to use the old insults until they became so familiar they lost their sting. I wanted to wallow in it, immerse myself in racism, I wanted to become *the* black the way Christ

195

was *the* man."

She burst into mocking laughter.

"Excuse me, but I couldn't help myself … You compare yourself to Christ; are you serious?"

"Every writer is Christ's competitor, if not his colleague. The idea of becoming a man to understand men, of suffering what they suffered to understand suffering, knowing the flesh to understand the wound of desire's arrows, dying to understand death, and being resurrected on the third day because you're the Creator and the whole thing was really only a game after all, a serious game, of course, but all the same … That's not so different from novel-writing."

She thought it over a minute, then told me, "Society should be allowed to throw people in jail for metaphors like that. Christ as a novelist—that's the limit! I know it's fashionable, but I find it totally unacceptable."

"Now, don't go and take it too seriously."

That was too much for her.

"First you compare yourself to Christ, then you want to be *the* black man as if there were never any black writers before you came along. You think you're suffering the worst torture in the world because you can't find the way to string words together the way you want to, then you tell me with a straight face not to take it too seriously. I'd really like to know who you are."

"I know what I'm *not* any more."

"Well, that's a start."

"*I'm not a black writer any more.*"

She smiled. There was a moment of silence.

"You're not a black writer any more?" she asked, half

196

amused, half astonished.

"No."

"You've given up on becoming the greatest black writer alive?"

"Yes."

"Then what's left?"

"Rest."

"There's no rest for the wicked."

"I suppose not."

"Good luck anyway," she said, kissing me on the cheek.

She turned down the next street. I stood there, frozen to the spot. Incredible, you spend your life on the run, in blind activity, thinking that time is yours forever, then one day, just like that, on a street corner, you have the most important conversation of your life with a nameless stranger.

"Oh, hell!"

I ran and caught up with her.

"Excuse me, but I didn't even think to ask you your name."

She turned around; it wasn't her. Another tall girl with black hair, liquid eyes and regular features. The same languid look that makes you wonder if she's sad or just shy. If you ask me, it's neither one nor the other. There must be millions like her in America.

The Assault on America

Here he comes, see him in the distance, practically dancing in his Reebok tennis shoes, the graceful bouncing move of the ghetto, a green and yellow beret sitting lightly on his head, the way the Rastamen wear them. His right arm swings, following the rhythm of his body. He's smiling, his face is relaxed, and that makes a contrast with the rest of his body, for he holds his torso in a state of tension, and his slender legs are slightly bent. A young animal about to spring or launch something. And what about that green thing he's holding? Is that a hand grenade or a piece of fruit?

BY THE SAME AUTHOR

How to Make Love to a Negro
Eroshima
An Aroma of Coffee
Dining with the Dictator

Coach House Press
50 Prince Arthur Avenue, Suite 107
Toronto, Canada M5R 1B5